MOONFELLOWS

DANGER SLATER

PMMP

Perpetual Motion Machine
Cibolo, Texas

Moonfellows
Copyright © 2022 Danger Slater

All Rights Reserved

ISBN: 978-1-943720-77-4

PERPETUAL MOTION MACHINE PUBLISHING

www.PerpetualPublishing.com

Cover by Matthew Revert

ALSO BY DANGER SLATER

I Will Rot Without You
Puppet Skin
He Digs a Hole
Impossible James

As the world keeps spinning
As I drift further away
I still think about you
All of you

*"Three things cannot be long hidden:
the sun, the moon, and the truth."*

—Buddha

THE MOONFELLOWS ARE:

Cpt. Dirk Mangrove—pilot

Dr. Kenji Tanaka—electronics and communications

Dr. Bethany Chase—geologist

Dr. Karishma 'Kari' Bhandary—engineer

—and lastly—

Franklin Crumb—excavation, and narrator of this book

1.

THERE ONCE WAS a man who lived on the moon.

My mother told this story to me often, back when I was just a boy. Though the details sometimes varied, that first line never changed.

She said the man on the moon lived in an old castle he fashioned for himself out of the rocks and the dust and debris. Whatever materials he could scavenge. Which wasn't much. He was alone and the moon was a desolate place.

But his castle had buttresses that extended like shoulder blades and spires like fingers that pointed straight up toward the star-freckled sky. The moon was as flat as a parking lot, my mother told me. It might've taken him a thousand years, but this man could construct his castle as large as he chose.

I once asked her how he got stuck on the moon in the first place.

She said the man had been up there forever. It was just the way things are. The way they always will be.

Some nights the wind would blow in off the Sasquahatchee River and rattle the sides of our cabin so hard it sounded like someone was slamming their fists against the door.

That's just the man on the moon breathing, my mother told me. All air comes from his lungs. It reminds us he's alive.

And when the clouds would roll in and the rain would fall, my mother said it was because the man on the moon was crying. She said his tears filled our streams and our lakes and our oceans. She said the man on the moon was sad. That he was *supposed* to be sad. That his sadness filled our well. So generous was his sorrow that nobody ever had to go thirsty. Because of him, plants grew. Fish swam. And whales hummed to each other beneath the sea.

When I huffed and puffed and refused to do my chores, my mother would remind me that the man on the moon was a giant with big googly eyes that bulged like periscopes out of his head. And from his castle he could see everything that I did, big and small. He knew all my secrets. She told me that if I didn't clean my room at least once a week, the man on the moon would reach his long, lanky arms down from the sky, snatch me out of my bed, and eat me while I slept.

I didn't like the idea of this strange man watching me all the time. Even in my most private moments. Even when I thought I was by myself. I begged my mother to protect me. To build our walls thicker so he couldn't see through them. But she would only laugh.

As long as I did as I was told, I'd always be safe, she assured me.

The man on the moon only ate messy children, she said.

Messy children tasted the best.

2.

MY MOTHER USED to tell me all kinds of tall tales. Allegories and legends of her own creation. She told me there was no use sticking to the old mythologies. She said you could build your own mythologies if you wanted. You could change the ending. You could rewrite history. You could fix all your mistakes.

My mother once told me that a story was a lie that told the truth.

I guess I'm still trying to figure out what she meant by that.

3.

THESE DAYS I can no longer remember my mother's face.

But when I close my eyes, I can sometimes still hear her voice.

I am not very clever. I don't have a lot of stories of my own.

In fact, looking back now, I only have one.

It began in the summer of 1906.

That was the year I married Bella.

That was also the year I was taken by the government against my will and sent on an ill-fated trip to the moon.

4.

NONE OF US had any idea what to expect once we got up there. We had our hypotheses, sure, but they were guesses at best. Our simple tools could only gather limited data. None of it provided us with much insight.

We assumed the moon was made of rock.

We assumed it was cold.

We assumed it was flat like a dinner plate and only a couple of miles wide. I mean, just look at it. It's tiny. Like an itty-bitty Frisbee stuck in the clouds.

But the truth was, all the training in the world would only take us so far. At the end of the day, there could be bug-eyed giants on the moon, just like my mother used to tell me as a kid. How could we know for certain until we saw for ourselves?

So, we were the first people in human history to travel beyond the troposphere. Into the parts of the sky heretofore unexplored. We were the pioneers of a dawning new age. The Space Age, we called it. It had a nice ring to it.

Yes, the moon was uncharted territory. And yes, the information we had going in was scant. But in light of all that, there was still one thing we knew for certain:

The mission was only supposed to last a few days. Enough to do some reconnaissance, extract the mineral samples we needed, and get the hell out. We weren't meant to stay up there forever. That wasn't part of the plan.

They called us the Moonfellow Five.

They said we'd be heroes. That we would conquer the stars.

We foolishly believed them. Right through to the bitter end.

No, the world does not function the same as a fairy tale. And the moon casts the same shadows on saints and sinners alike. I know that everything I'm about to tell you will sound like bullshit. And I know you have no reason to believe anything I say. But I have no ulterior motives. I'm not here to proselytize. I'm not looking to entertain you. I don't even want your money. I have no use for money on the moon.

My point is, so what if the chronology doesn't add up? And who cares if the science doesn't make any sense? We didn't have the technology for space travel back in 1906, you say? Well I'd hate to be one to burst your skeptical little bubble, but everything I'm about to tell you is the hand-to-god truth. So just listen.

The Moonfellow Program was never disclosed to the public. And our records have been long since black-barred and sealed. The government wasted millions of dollars just to get us up here. It was a blunder of unprecedented proportions, and for the red-handed parties who remained back on Earth, it was just easier to pretend like the whole thing never happened.

"The Moonfellows? Nope. Never heard of 'em. Sounds made-up to me."

The existence of my four crewmates and I have been completely expunged from the record books. And everything we went through will be forgotten to time. I am going to die. Alone. In space.

So tell me, does *that* sound like the start of a fucking fairy tale to you?

5.

THE OTHER MOONFELLOWS were exactly the types of people you'd assume would be recruited for a mission like this. Strong. Canny. Educated. Resourceful. Between them lay a broad array of highly specialized skills, against which someone like me could never compare. I couldn't fly a spaceship. Or build a rocket booster. Or wire up a telecommunications device that could keep us in contact with the people back on Earth. I couldn't even fry up an egg without breaking the yolk. I've heard the trick is to use low heat, but I've never been able to get it quite right.

I didn't bring much to the team in the practical sense. I wasn't a scientist. I didn't even graduate high school. I was less like a peer and more like a tool. Like a screwdriver. Or a toothpick. Something brought along to accomplish a specific task. I believe this is why President Harper sought me out in the first place. I had no philosophical insights. No technical expertise. No formal training of any kind.

I was just really good at digging graves.

6.

BEFORE THE DAY I met the other Moonfellows, my world was much more uncomplicated.

I wasn't a spaceman yet. I wasn't anything at all. Life was easy. And things were good.

My last day at home started like any other. I woke up in my own bed. In my own house. In my sleepy little suburban New Jersey town. Rays of honey-colored sunshine gently cajoled me into consciousness. It was late summer. A cloudless sky. As nice a day as any you could ask for.

A cup of hot black coffee. The steam in my nostrils and bitter taste on my tongue. I sat alone at the table while my wife and daughter still slept in the back room. Bella and I had only been married 6 months at that point. Our relationship still as fresh as the dew that accompanied the dawn.

Morning used to be my favorite part of the day. Before work. Before chores. Before the thousands of other things that demanded my attention. Just me and my newspaper and my thoughts. The quiet. The solitude. Ironic to think about now. On the moon I have solitude in a constant supply.

When I finished my coffee, I rinsed out the mug. I put on my overalls. Strapped on my boots. Grabbed my trusty old shovel. And I crept out of the house, gently closing the door behind me so as not to wake anyone else.

MOONFELLOWS

It was a half-mile walk to the Lone Fir Cemetery. The largest cemetery in town. And I already knew I had a long day ahead of me. Yesterday morning a commuter train derailed. It flipped off the track and tumbled into the river. Car after car. Piled up like matchsticks. Blood flowed from the wreckage and organs and entrails billowed up the water like sea foam. I was told the Sasquahatchee still ran red.

There were a *lot* of casualties. And they all had to be buried. I got paid per hole. It was backbreaking work. But I was making good money.

The sun eventually got low. Dusk settled in like a bruise. I brushed off my pants and knocked the mud off my shoes. The headstones surrounded me like mushroom caps as I walked home. I dug twenty-five graves that day. Not my personal best, but close.

I arrived to find the dinner table already set. Napkins and silverware and a basket full of semi-sweet rolls. I plopped down on my seat between Bella and Maxine. My five-month-old daughter was still too young to talk, but she smiled a lot for a baby as she took in the room with her curiously wide eyes. I'd make a monkey face and she'd laugh. I'd make an alligator face and she'd squeal and turn away. It was our little game. Our secret little conversation.

"So how was your day, dear?" Bella asked.

"It was good," I replied, as I filled my bowl with a ladle of beef stew. "That train accident has been keepin' me busy. Another railway disaster like that and we might be able to afford a second kid sooner than we thought. Would you like that, Maxine? A baby brother or sister?"

Maxine cooed. I chuckled. Everything was perfect. And then there came a knock on the door.

rap rap

A heavy fist. Not very polite. Someone wanted to make damn sure we heard them.

"You expecting visitors, Frankie?" Bella asked.

I placed my spoon down. "No, were you?"

9

She opened it and was met on the other side by two wide-shouldered men in matching black suits, looking as cold and impassive as the rocks in the garden.

They might've been identical twins had the one not stood a head taller than his stouter companion. They both wore square-framed sunglasses even though it was already past dark. Their brown hair was cropped and cut short. They were clean-shaven. Pale-skinned. Box-jawed.

"Is this the residence of Franklin Rutherford Crumb?" the short one asked.

"Rutherford?" asked Bella. I guess I never told her my middle name.

"Franklin Rutherford Crumb. Age: 27. Height: 5 foot 11. Occupation: groundskeeper and gravedigger at the Lone Fir Cemetery, Sasquahatchee, New Jersey?"

"Is there a problem . . . um . . . officers?"

"No problem at all, ma'am. In fact, we'll only be a minute. This is a matter of national security. We are authorized to use deadly force if necessary, so please remain calm."

They pushed their way past her and barreled into the house.

"Ooh, is that beef stew?" the lanky one asked.

"Not now, Higgins," the short one said.

"It smells delicious, though, boss."

"Higgins, not now!"

I sprang up as the secret servicemen closed in on me from either side. My back hit the wall and a vase fell off the mantle and shattered against the floor. I looked at the table. A single butter knife sat next to my plate. What was I going to do with that? Spread jam on their muffins? Even if it had been a battleaxe, I wouldn't have had enough time to grab it, anyway.

"What is the meaning of this?" I said. Voice already starting to crack. There was no place to run.

"There's no reason to be alarmed, Mr. Crumb," Higgins

said, as he grabbed me by the wrist and quickly spun me around in some sort of fancy taekwondo takedown maneuver. Pain shot through my arm and I dropped to my knees.

Bella scooped Maxine out of her highchair and they retreated to the opposite side of the room. Tears streamed down her face. The infant wailed.

"What is happening?!" Bella cried. "Franklin, what the hell is going on?!"

"We're here under the authority of the United States Government," the short man said, as he cuffed my hands behind my back.

"What for?" I demanded.

"I'm afraid that's classified," he replied.

"Classified my ass! I know my rights!" I screamed and thrashed, but it was no use. "You can't do this! I pay my taxes! Get your goddamn hands off me!"

"I'm afraid your presence is mandatory, Mr. Crumb. Thank you for your compliance."

"Yeah, and we're *also* gonna need to commandeer some of that beef stew . . . " Higgins winked at my wife. " . . . to go."

7.

THEY SLIPPED A blindfold over my eyes. I could hear Bella begging them to let me go, but they paid her no mind. Maxine bawled into her mother's shoulder. I tried to keep my voice calm for her. For the both of them.

"It's okay," I said to my family. "Everything is gonna be fine."

In the backseat of a mobile carriage I was placed. Squished between the two agents. So tight our shoulders touched. I could smell my wife's stew on Higgins' breath.

The carriage started moving down the mottled path. Away from my home. Bella's cries quickly faded into the night. And I demanded of my captors:

"Where are we going?"

—and—

"Why is this happening?"

—and—

"Under whose command are you acting upon?"

But the two men refused to answer my questions.

And eventually, I stopped asking them.

8.

HOURS PASSED, though I couldn't be sure of how many. These bumpy country roads made for a sleepless ride. When the cloth around my eyes was finally removed, I was assaulted by the full force of the noonday sun. It took a few blinks before my vision returned to normal.

"What the hell is this?"

No answer.

"Are we in Washington DC?"

Still no answer.

"I know we're in DC, okay? I can see the Capitol Building right over there."

"Okay, fine, we're in DC," the short one conceded. "Happy? Now for the love of god, will you please shut up?"

"No, I'm not happy! And no, I won't shut up. Why did you blindfold me if you were just going to take me somewhere I'd instantly recognize? Is this your first day on the job? Doesn't that defeat the whole purpose?"

"Look, dude, I don't know what to tell ya. The whole blindfold thing was Higgins' idea."

"What?! No way, that was totally your idea, man!"

9.

I SUSPECTED THE other four Moonfellows found themselves "persuaded" to join the agents in much the same manner that I was, because we soon found ourselves lined up together on the White House lawn. Exhausted and intimidated and desperate for an explanation.

Black-suited servicemen were posted around us like croquet wickets. As still as statues. Not a single smirker in the bunch. Not even Higgins. This was official business. As official as it gets.

And soon enough, there stood the man himself, Archibald Eugene Harper III, the 26th President of the United States of America, his long limbs casting long shadows around us, as imposing and unreal as I ever imagined him. Looking like royalty. Looking like he just stepped off a $20 bill.

An American flag thwipped at the top of a nearby pole as the breeze sent the petals of the magnolia trees aflutter. Yet not a hair dared sway on President Harper's head. His skin was tan and his hands were big and his unflappable voice was punctuated by the bushy gray mustache on his upper lip.

"Wow, y'all look like you're about to soil your collective britches," he chuckled. "It's okay. You're safe. You're at the White House. This is probably the safest place there is. I know this whole situation is all very jarring. You probably didn't get very much sleep last night, and now you're standing here talking to the President of the goddamn United States of goddamn America. This must certainly be a great honor for you. Yadayadayada. I'll be honest, I hear this kinda shit every day. So let's skip the formalities and get down to brass tacks, shall we? What I'm about to tell you is highly classified information. I'm talkin' top-secret, highest-echelon level stuff. Suffice it to say, mums-the-word here. Lest you want a bullet in the head. Folks, the United States Government needs your assistance. The future of your country—and quite possibly the world—may depend on it."

The five of us exchanged nervous glances. Dubious of each other. Dubious of everything. But President Harper smiled. Lips curled out from beneath those whiskers of his. An expression somehow both capricious and avuncular. Calculated but affable. He was polished. Like all politicians.

With a quick nod, he motioned to a pair of nearby guards. Nobody said a word as the two men struggled to wheel a wooden rack across the grass towards the waiting Commander.

On its shelves sat an assortment of different types of weaponry. There were guns of various calibers and a huge selection of knives. High-grade rifles. Blunderbusses. Samurai swords. Letter openers. Grenades. Throwing stars. Tomahawks. Even a couple medieval maces.

President Harper took a moment to browse before settling on a large machete.

Sunlight bounced off the tip of the blade as he slashed at the air, testing the feel of it. When he seemed satisfied, the rack was squeakily wheeled away.

A few seconds later, another agent made his way across the lawn, this time towing a massive wide-antlered moose on a leash behind him.

President Harper stroked the nose of the animal as he addressed the five of us.

"Look, I realize this meeting has been somewhat

unorthodox. Believe it or not, the US Government doesn't typically go around kidnapping people all willy-nilly, and my men aren't exactly trained in the art of coercion and subtlety. Unlike me. I've been told I'm an excellent negotiator. Perhaps a quick demonstration of my negotiation skills would help to alleviate some of your concerns."

He swung the machete into the side of the moose's head, splitting it open with a wet crack. The beast brayed and bellowed and kicked its hind legs, but the servicemen held the leash tight and kept it from fighting back.

Brain matter sloshed out of the hole. The broad blade was covered in blood. The President raised the machete over his head and swung it down again. And again. And again. He was screaming like a maniac as he bushwhacked his way into the animal, so loud and intense it almost sounded like he was having an orgasm.

The other Moonfellows recoiled. A few looked sick. Even I had to look away. This creature was unraveling before our very eyes. Fleshy chunk by fleshy chunk. Its face. Its side. Its back. Its legs. In pieces. Globs of pink gore puddled up in the grass around us until the moose *finally* collapsed into a pile of butchered body parts. Dead.

The President of the United States let out one last grunt. We could see the cum stain soaking through the front of his slacks.

"Man, that's the stuff. Someone go get me a towel," he said to one of the servicemen. He kicked the dead animal. "And get this nasty-ass thing outta here while you're at it." President Harper turned to us. His eyes shone like pearls in the middle of his blood-spattered face. "Stupid moose. You can't trust 'em. They come from the north. Canada mostly. The Arctic territories. Sometimes even Russia. Theory is that they use natural rafts. Floatin' across the Bering Strait on pieces of driftwood an' shit. Just imagine you're out there fishing on your little boat an' all of a sudden this moose is coming straight at you in a fuckin' log canoe. You gotta always be on guard. Your enemies might be lurking in your own backyard."

A serviceman grabbed the animal by the antlers and pulled until its head came completely off its body. He stuck it on the end of a pike on the edge of the property for the tourists on Pennsylvania Avenue to see.

"Speak softly and carry a big stick. That's the best advice I could give you." The President wiped his face clean and leaned in. Closely. Conspiratorially. His voice was barely above a whisper as he continued. "Look, I don't need to waste any more time with metaphors, do I? I singled y'all out. I tracked y'all down. I brought y'all here for a reason. So here are the facts. We've recently discovered something. Something important. Something big. Something that has the potential to change the world as we know it and put the United States of America technologically beyond what we ever thought possible. Something that'll act as a machete right into the unsuspecting neck of the future."

"And what is that?" the big guy to my right asked. This was Dirk Mangrove. The man brought aboard to be our mission captain.

President Harper reached into his pocket and pulled out a tiny 2-carat gem. About the size of a marble. He held it out for us to inspect.

"This, my friends, is MacGuffinite."

He tossed it to the slender woman to my left. Dr. Bethany Chase. The geologist. She caught it and raised it up to the light. Her eyes went wide. Mouth fell agape. Transfixed by the twinkling stone as if she'd been hypnotized.

"What the hell is MacGuffinite?" she asked. "Where did you find this?"

President Harper extended a single finger and pointed at the sky.

10.

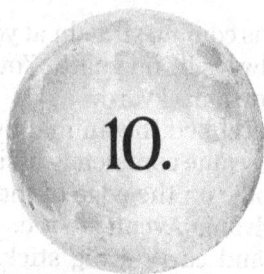

SO I IMAGINE you have a lot of questions.

I had a lot of questions myself, once upon a time.

There are lots of smart people in the world, but I've never been one of them. I figured those who acted like they had all the answers must've known something I didn't.

Where should I dig?

How deep should I dig?

Would you gentlemen with the guns like me to keep digging?

I wasn't authorized to ask anything else.

I suppose we got lucky. If you could consider any of this luck. The oxygen levels on the moon were at a tolerable level. Were it not for that, I doubt we would've lasted five minutes. Our ship was broken and our suits were breached. I've heard the air on Venus is made of sulfur dioxide. But on the moon, the air wasn't bad at all. It whipped across the surface of the planet just like it did on Earth. A little chilly at times. And a little thin. It felt like the breeze at the top of a tall mountain. Or perhaps like the wind that swirled around arctic poles. Not quite the Bahamas. But it was still good ole fashioned O_2. As much as we'd ever need. In and out of our lungs.

Our first few weeks on the moon, and we still hadn't found any MacGuffinite yet. Not a single nugget. Not a solitary grain. Initial reports told us this place should've been teeming with it. Overflowing with it. Pockets of

MacGuffinite should've been waiting for us just below the moonscape, ready to geyser up with the slightest of pricks.

I dug my holes as instructed. I dug them wide and deep. I dug holes so big you might've mistaken them for meteor strikes. I was truly functioning at the top of my game. My old boss at the Lone Fir would've been proud.

Yet all we found was dust. Lots and lots and lots of dust.

"So you know how the molecular structure of a diamond contains five tightly packed covalent carbon atoms arranged within a tetrahedral lattice?" Dr. Chase once asked me. She'd brought that marble-sized sample of MacGuffinite with her to the moon and continued to study it, even after we crashed. Of course, this was right before we discovered the full extent of the sublunar-time dilation. And the Moon Flu. And all the mysterious secrets that lurked on the dark side. Right before everything *really* got hopeless and dark and weird. "Well when it comes to MacGuffinite, those numbers are nearly doubled! As far as these kinds of allotropes go, I've never seen anything quite like it. I mean, the thermionic emission point on it alone is off the charts. This might be the most versatile substance ever discovered. The potential uses here are as vast as they are varied."

I had no idea what she was talking about. But I played along.

"Do you think this MacGuffinite stuff can help us get off the moon?"

"I think it can do a hella lot more than that."

I cocked an eyebrow. She pointed to our busted ship.

"With just a slight modification to the chemical composition, you'd be able to quickly and cost-effectively transform MacGuffinite into a sort of nearly-indestructible lightweight thermoplastic. It would make an ideal building material for things like aeroplanes and submarines."

"And spaceships?" I asked.

Dr. Chase nodded. "Yeah. And spaceships too. I'm telling you, Crumb, this stuff is safe and cheap and an excellent insulator to boot. I'm talking about a 98% heat retention/repulsion rate. Heat. Cold. Wouldn't make a difference. And it looks like with just another little molecular tweak, you could flip that number around and have it burn clean, too."

"Burn clean?"

"As opposed to coal or any other combustion-based fossil fuels. MacGuffoline™ we could call it. In fact, I'm trademarking the name right now. This stuff could reinvigorate economic trade routes and reinvent commercial travel with no negative ecological impact whatsoever. I'm beginning to see why the President sent us up here. Whoever controls the supply of this stuff would, in effect, control the future. Now come here and take a look at this. I wanna show you something else."

I peered into the microscope and almost blinded myself.

"Ah shit. It's . . . uh . . . certainly *shiny* . . ."

"Of course it's shiny. It has exceptional conductive properties."

"Conductive? Like telephone lines or something?"

"Crumb, this stuff is gonna make telephone lines look like wet spaghetti."

"Did someone say spaghetti?" Captain Mangrove called out from the other side of the site. "You guys got spaghetti over there? Quit holdin' out on me."

Dr. Chase ignored him and pressed on. "I have this crazy idea. I was thinking about MacGuffinite cables. How we could use 'em to concentrate and transmit different waves of light. Like *fibers* of *optics*. Almost like electric signals. But much faster. And with the capacity to hold much more data. I'm talking communication. Entertainment. Banking. Everything. A literal *information superhighway* that anyone with an access terminal would be able to *surf*, all of which would be stored within an interconnected network of shared devices. An *internet*, if you will. Perhaps we could even implement a kinda of *engine* to help make this *internet* more *searchable*. Kinda like a digital butler that we could summon with a *yahoo*! I mean, we're talking the entire compendium of human knowledge here. There could be *googols* of pages to comb through. It'd be nice to simply *ask Jeeves* to fetch it for us. Before the clock could go *tik tok*, it'd be like *bing* here you go. A recipe for watermelon salad. Or tentacle hentai. Whatever you need at the touch of a button."

"Blah blah freakin' blah," Mangrove huffed. "Like anyone is ever gonna care about something with a stupid name like the *internet*. Now answer my question, doc. Can we eat this stuff or not?"

"I would not recommend it. No."

"Bah. Whatever. Sounds like a buncha alarmist bullshit to me. I mean, I've seen your little sample there. It looks just like rock candy. I bet it tastes just like lemonade."

"Please do not eat my sample, Captain Mangrove."

"Don't forget I'm the leader of this mission, Dr. Chase. I'll eat whatever I goddamn please."

11.

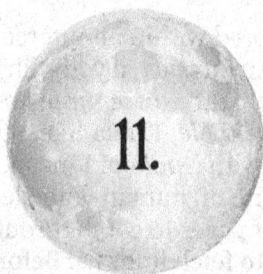

THE MOON SLUGS showed up almost immediately after the crash and have remained ever-present since.

We didn't know where they came from or how they managed to survive on the desolate lunar surface alone. But there were millions of them, worming their way through the dust. They were the only living creatures to greet us upon our arrival. The only other living creatures on the moon beside us.

Captain Mangrove was the first of us to spot one. This was only a few minutes after we climbed out of the twisted wreckage of the destroyed ship.

"Holy shit! Aliens! I've discovered aliens!"

We rushed over to where Mangrove was standing. Dozens of slugs surrounded him. They oozed their way across the ground. Crisscrossing trails of wet mucus in their wake.

"What the *fuck*?" said Dr. Tanaka.

Captain Mangrove scooped one up. Held it in the palm of his hand.

"I'm gonna be famous," he said. "Like, even more famous than the rest of you chumps. You can have the credit for that MacGuffinite crap. I don't care. I'm gonna be the dude who made first contact with an alien species! Wow!"

He tickled the slug on the belly like it was a baby.

"Coochie-coo. Coochie-choochie-coo."

MOONFELLOWS

All six inches of it curled around the tip of his finger. The color of pond water. Freckled by black spots. I leaned in close. Nearly touching it with my nose. Its dark eyes were like tulip bulbs, set upon a pair of periscope-like stalks. The creature regarded me with disinterest.

"*Limax maximus*," I said.

"*Gesundheit*," Mangrove replied.

"No. The thing in your hand. It's not an alien. It's a *limax maximus*. A leopard slug."

"What the hell are you talking about, Crumb?"

"They're fairly common back on Earth. I'd see 'em at the Lone Fir all the time. Climbing on the tombstones. Or tucked away in the grass. They're garden slugs. Just like we got in New Jersey. Completely run-of-the-mill."

"Garden slugs?"

"Yeah."

"On the moon?"

" . . . yeah?"

"I'm sorry, but do you see any fuckin' gardens around here, Crumb?"

"That's just what they're called, sir. It's a colloquialism. Like how a banana fish isn't made out of an actual banana."

Captain Mangrove looked like he wanted to hit me. I slowly backed off. I didn't have any more answers for him. I didn't have any answers for any of them. I wasn't even sure about that banana fish fact I just dropped. Maybe it was half-banana. What the hell did I know. These people were scientists. They were supposed to tell *me* things. Not the other way around.

23

12.

THE SLUGS SLITHERED by with a surprising degree of regularity. Moving waves, as if controlled by unseen cosmic forces. Almost like the tides. There was never a shortage of them. This was their world. No matter where you went. No matter what you did. There they were. We learned to ignore them. Just like we would've back on Earth.

Quickly, we were running out of provisions. But we did what we could to facilitate our rescue. We tried to stay positive. We didn't know it then, but we were already fucked.

Dr. Tanaka tinkered with the damaged communications systems. Crossed wires and soldered fuses. It only had to work once, he said. A single blip on a solitary screen. *Beep.* SOS. We're out here. We're still alive. I'm sorry we haven't found any MacGuffinite yet. I promise I'll keep looking. Please send another ship to pick us up. Have them bring sandwiches. Pastrami.

Dr. Bhandary worked on the ship. Our resources were scant, but she did what she could. Repurposed the scrap and assorted debris to try and patch up the hull of our formerly spaceworthy vessel. "Hopeful" was her succinct reply when I once asked her how things were coming along, though there was something about her tone that made me wonder if she were telling the truth.

Dr. Chase turned her focus from the MacGuffinite to

the moon slugs. Trying to figure out what they were surviving on. And how. She was no biologist, but she did her best. She had a theory about the soil. How it might've contained trace elements of some essential vitamins and minerals. Just enough to sustain life. The slugs apparently didn't need food or water. They could just eat the dirt.

"That's all well and good, Dr. Chase, but what does it *taste* like?" Captain Mangrove asked. "I have a very discerning palate. My father was a sommelier."

"Please don't eat the dirt, sir. We don't know what we're dealing with yet."

"Okay. Fine. No eating the dirt." Mangrove scooped up a pinkyful of moon dust and tooted it up his nose instead. He cock-a-doodle-dooed like a rooster. "Goddamn, that's good stuff! These slugs know what's up. They're smarter than they look."

We didn't know it, but Captain Mangrove was already well in the throes of the Moon Flu then, though he was not yet exhibiting any of its more extreme symptoms. We'd noticed his behavior had grown somewhat erratic. And he'd been looking a little strange. But the disease hadn't yet boiled his brain. Nor had it warped his genes beyond recognition. We'd all gone a little mad over the past few weeks. It didn't mean he was dangerous.

"Call me a romantic but I find the moon kind of serene," he said to me one evening, the two of us tucked in our cots, the rest of the team already asleep. "I feel like I can really let my hair down, ya know? I can take off the mask. I can finally be myself."

"Are you—*masturbating*—right now, sir?"

"Yes. And don't make it weird, Crumb. Now let me put a finger in your mouth. I promise this'll only take a few minutes."

13.

BUT THAT WAS all months away. We still had a lot of work to do. Whether we wanted to or not.

The President of the United States of America went back inside. He didn't say goodbye and neither did we. There was no pomp. No pageantry. Nobody even gave us napkins to clean the moose blood off ourselves. The sun fell behind a gray cloud. And just like that, the meeting was over.

We were herded off the White House lawn and corralled into the backseat of a horse-drawn carriage, which giddy-upped its way down Pennsylvania Avenue and quickly out of town. Higgins and his stouter partner joined the driver up front. Our armed escorts. Our prison guards. Higgins hummed Beethoven's "Moonlight Sonata" softly to himself for most of the ride. It might've been hauntingly prophetic if it hadn't been so off-key.

All signs of civilization soon tapered down. Uninhabited woodland consumed the cityscape. There were signposts to guide our way. The road was not paved. We bounced across the hillside for nearly an hour until we came upon a massive beige warehouse, incongruous amid the trees.

"I didn't know they could make buildings this big," Dr. Bhandary said to me, her eyes wide like milk vats, seemingly more curious than terrified at the prospect of going inside it. It was the first words any of the

MOONFELLOWS

Moonfellows had spoken directly to me. I was not expecting it.

"Ayup" was all I could dumbly reply, like my tongue was a frog that had died in my mouth.

The structure before us bore no identifying markings. No symbols. No street address. Hell, it wasn't even on a street. The underbrush overtook the trail from where we came, forest upon forest layered so thick it was almost like a wall. I'm sure this place wasn't listed in the phone book or drawn into any sort of map. We were in the middle of goddamn nowhere.

The carriage stopped in front of a singular nondescript door, painted the same color as the rest of the building. The only entrance along its entire façade. A sharp-looking government liaison stood beside it, hair slicked back so tightly that his skin was pulled taut. Smiling as we approached. Waiting for us to pile out. We lined up and faced our handsome new captor and the imposing structure behind him. He held out his arms wide like he was expecting a hug.

"Welcome to your last home on Earth," he said.

14.

WE ENTERED THE warehouse and were immediately swallowed whole.

A few feet in and it somehow felt as if we'd already wandered for miles.

Walls stretched across four opposing horizons, so far apart that the room seemed to curve. Cavernous ceilings were salted by skylights and tic-tac-toed by support beams. The cadaver-gray concrete underfoot looked like a frozen ocean. Even the air around us felt prepackaged. As if it was new. Both in design and in scope, this building was a marvel.

The warehouse was divided into multiple sections, although their demarcation was often unclear. Some tape on the floor stretched out in thin lines were all we had to navigate with. Different areas had been set up to take care of whatever amenities we'd require:

There were sleeping quarters.

Living/dining spaces.

Five separate training grounds, tailored to each person's specific disciplines and needs.

A mechanics bay with all the latest tools readily available.

Shower stalls.

Toilet stalls.

Muttering-and-weeping-quietly-to-yourself   stalls. Although those were labeled as 'mental health cubbies'.

There were office cubicles set up in one corner of the room and a large computer console taking up most of the wall. I had never seen a computer before. I had never even heard of such a contraption. But here was one now that we could use at our discretion. It was as big as a house and full of blinking lights, rotating widgets, steaming vents, and beeping oscilloscopes.

"What does that do?" Dr. Tanaka asked the liaison giving us the tour.

The liaison raised a manicured eyebrow and said "lemme show you" as he walked up to the machine and pressed a small, red button on its side.

The computer clunked and whizzed and whirred. A sustained honk like an air raid siren rang out. I covered my ears as the entire warehouse shook upon its foundation. It was like thunder. Like tectonic plates shifting. Like the end of the world. I looked over and saw a terrified Dr. Chase. Her eyes were squeezed shut and she was silently praying to herself for it to end.

And it finally did.

38 minutes later.

A bell went *ping* and a panel on the side of the console opened, from which the liaison took out a cup of steaming coffee and gave us a little 'cheers' before taking a sip.

"Makes it fresh and hot, every time," he said.

The five of us *oohed* and *aahed*.

15.

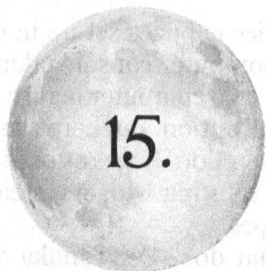

NONE OF US had any bags or personal belongings. We were taken from our homes without warning or time to prepare. But there were five cots lined up. One for each of us. Each with a light blue canvas jumpsuit lain out on top of it. Our uniforms.

I picked mine up and gave it the once over. Above the breast pocket was a sheet of paper loosely pinned on it that read: EMBROIDER NAME HERE.

We were in a top-secret facility. Like Area 51. Except you've probably heard of Area 51, so that's not really a great example. This place was *more* secret than Area 51. So maybe like, I don't know, Area 4 or something like that. Area X, let's call it. Yeah, that sounds cool.

In here we were expected to learn to work together and prepare for the upcoming mission. We'd each been ~~kidnapped~~ drafted by the US Government because we were the best at what we did, but as the billboard-sized banner that hung from the ceiling constantly reminded us:

WORK HARDER!
YOU CAN ALWAYS DO BETTER

Higgins and a bunch of the other armed guards were posted throughout the room and made sure we were always "training with enthusiasm" as President Harper put it.

"Enthusiasm is one of our country's greatest resources," the President said. "Go to Estonia or Belarus or one of those godforsaken places. No one in Europe has been happy for over 1000 years. That's why the pilgrims set sail in the first place. They wanted to get their groove back. The five of you should be counting your lucky stars you were born in the good ole U.S.A. There are people all over the globe who only ever get to experience joy when they're watching an American-made talking picture show. Let that sink in, you privileged fucks."

I didn't know there was even a country *called* Belarus, but I was in no position to question him. This man was the President of the United States, after all. I figured there must have been some kind of geography test he had to pass before taking office.

Harper said we should be proud of the sacrifices we were making. He said we were patriots. He said we should smile more. He said smiles were now mandatory. Another banner above read as such:

SMILE OR ELSE

The liaison pointed to the janitor closet and told us anyone caught frowning would have to spend the night in the attitude adjustment chamber thinking about what they'd done.

16.

AND SO THIS unmarked warehouse in the middle of the woods became a hive of government-sanctioned clandestine activity. Nobody complained. Everyone put on a happy face. And each of us worked thanklessly on our respective assignments.

Captain Mangrove built himself a practice cockpit out of the basin of an old bathtub he dragged from one of the supply rooms. He installed a padded seat and steering wheel inside it and welded a bunch of scrap metal onto the cast iron frame to act as different gauges.

I pointed at one of the big switches on the right. "So what does this button do?"

He swatted my hand away. "It doesn't do anything. None of them do anything. But I assume the actual cockpit will have a buncha instrumentation that looks like this. Figured I might as well stick some in my practice tub and get used to it."

He blindly mashed at his useless dashboard while making honking sound effects with his mouth.

"Hey do me a favor, Crumb. Pretend to be a meteor."

"What?"

"A meteor. Like you'd find in space. They're gonna be coming at us left and right up there. Jeezus, man, would you stop arguing with me for like two friggin' seconds? I'm the goddamn captain of this ship. *Lives* are at stake here!"

"Okay, okay," I said, as I took a few steps back. I tucked

my head into my arms and hunched my back to make myself as meteor-ish as possible. I slowly walked toward him.

"Uhh, does this work?" I asked.

"Oh shit, it's a motherfuckin' *meteor*!" he shouted. "I'm going to need to do evasive maneuvers! Zoooommmmmm! Hit the boosters! Man the torpedoes! Warp drive!"

Later that day, he suspended his makeshift cockpit from an industrial-sized ceiling fan with a set of rickety chains. He claimed this was to simulate the centrifugal force we would experience when leaving the Earth's atmosphere.

He sat in his bathtub and turned the fan on and spun around and around and around and around, laughing like a child the entire time.

Not far away, Dr. Chase sat hunched over a well-lit table, a retaining wall of microscopes and Bunsen burners arranged in a semi-circle around her.

The geologist placed the MacGuffinite sample on a slide. Peered into the magnifying tube. She shook her head like a schoolmarm admonishing an ill-behaved child.

tsk tsk tsk

"Problem?" I asked.

"Lots of them," she replied. "Lots to still figure out. Lots to learn."

"How did the MacGuffinite get to Earth in the first place? I mean, if it's supposedly only on the moon, where did this sample even come from?"

"Well, I imagine it must've been ejected through some natural process. A *cratering event* or something along those lines. That's the leading theory, at least."

"A cratering event?"

"Yeah, like a collision with an asteroid or some large piece of celestial debris. The force of the impact would've sent fragments of the lunar surface hurtling out into space. And since the Earth sits *below* the moon, it only stands to reason, this is where they would've fallen."

"Kinda like rain?"

"Yeah. Kinda. Though in this case it's more like a singular raindrop. The rarest, most expensive, and most chemically complex raindrop ever discovered."

She looked back into her microscope and went *tsk tsk tsk* again.

At the other end of the facility, Dr. Tanaka was developing a new kind of communications system. One that claimed could withstand the rigors of space travel.

"Hey, Crumb. Come here. I want to show you something cool."

I walked toward his workstation, a mess of tangled wires and half-fused metals, among which were the two complementary devices he built.

The first was a geodesic sphere. Roughly the size of a tractor wheel. Thousands of small mirrored panels covered its surface like dragon scales. I could see my reflection stretched like taffy upon it. A contorted mass of limbs and flesh that only vaguely resembled Franklin Crumb.

The second device was smaller than the first. Perhaps the size of a pinball machine. A glass screen was encased inside of a wooden box. Vacuum tubes poked out of the back. A typewriter was attached to the front. Exposed cables were wrapped haphazardly around the whole thing—battery glued to one side, telephone receiver glued to the other. A two-foot-long pointy antenna stuck out of the top like the saber of a cavalry leader as he led the charge into battle.

It looked like a pile of garbage to me, but Dr. Tanaka was beaming with pride as he explained the logistics of whatever-the-fuck this contraption was.

"I call it a 'sat-e-lite telecaster,'" he said.

"A sat-e-lite telecaster?"

"Yessir. And it's actually pretty simple, all things considered. I'm legit surprised I'm the first person to think of it. You see, all we have to do is cast this mirrored ball thingy out of the ship after we break free from the atmosphere. It honestly doesn't matter where exactly. As long as we're up high enough to leave it in orbit. Like a tiny little moon itself. From there, we should be able to control the sat-e-lite through an electronic signal transmitted through this smaller-looking doohickey right here. Using this typewriter, I can punch in the location for anywhere on Earth and the mirrors on it'll whirr and purr and rearrange themselves to reflect to us whatever is happening in that exact spot. Then the image will be projected to us in real-time via the glass screen that I'm calling a *tele-vision*."

"Tele-vision," I parroted him again. I was learning a lot of new words.

"Think of it like a *big eye* in the *sky*," Dr. Tanaka said. "Hell, if the person we're looking at has got a telephone nearby—or theoretically, another sat-e-lite telecaster, which is impossible, of course, since I only built this one— then we can actually use it to *call* them and talk directly. What I'm sayin' is, with this machine, we can stay in constant contact with the Earth no matter how far away we go."

And Dr. Bhandary was, of course, the busiest of all. The project engineer. Construction of the spaceship was under her command.

She'd been tackling it in parts. One section at a time, to be assembled later. The curved steel plates that would reinforce the hull, layered around the vessel like a coat of paint. The foot-thick windshield that would make up the front of our craft. The smaller porthole-sized ones that would run along the starboard side. And the piece she was currently working on. Perhaps the most important piece of all. The rocket booster.

The large dangerous tube smelled like kerosene and campfire. And although it must have weighed several tons, it was suspended from the ceiling by only a few flimsy leather straps. A claustrophobic foot-and-a-half gap separated the bottom of the booster from the floor. Dr. Bhandary's two skinny legs stuck out from underneath it like raspberry brambles.

As I got close, the constant *clug clug clug* of her hammer suddenly stopped and her velvet voice called out to me. "Ratchet."

"Huh?" I absently said, after a brief pause. I didn't even know she knew I was there.

She slid out on a rolling stool, grease smeared on her face and clumped in her hair. "You just gonna stand there looking stupid, Crumb, or are you gonna hand me the ratchet?"

I grabbed what I thought was a ratchet from a nearby toolbox.

"That's a wrench," she said.

"I know that," I replied. Which, of course, I didn't.

She stood up, sauntered over, and reached into the toolbox herself, producing a tool that looked suspiciously similar to a wrench to me.

She held it up so I could take note.

Then she wheeled herself back under the vessel and resumed banging away.

17.

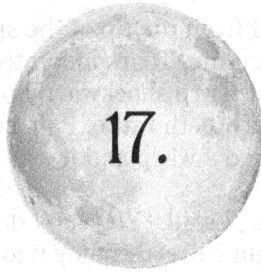

A 10x10 SQUARE partitioned off by yellow caution tape, inside of which was nothing but a thick concrete slab. I was handed a shovel by the liaison. He motioned toward the floor.

"So what the hell ya waitin' for, Crumb? An invitation from the queen? Get diggin'."

The ground was solid as a rock. The ground literally *was* a rock. I wasn't sure what he expected of me. Even the frozenest dirt in the middle of the New Jerseyest winter would be like a cakewalk when compared to this.

"Uh, this is concrete, sir. It's specifically designed to be *undiggable*. In fact, that's pretty much its only attribute. It's how they market it."

"I guess you're just gonna hafta work a little extra hard then, aren't ya, Crumb?"

"Sir . . . "

"Look, the moon may be made of quicksand. Or it may be made of solid quartz. We won't know until we get there. You're just gonna hafta be prepared to get through it, either way. That's why we brought you here. So stop being a whiny little bitch and do what I'm telling you to do, okay?"

The liaison flashed me a shark-toothed smile. What choice did I have? In one smooth chopping motion, I swung the shovel straight down into the concrete as hard as I could.

clink

Sparks shot out from the tip of the spade. It felt like a lightning bolt struck me. Tears instantly streamed down my face. The impact sent a shockwave rippling through my body. I could feel my teeth rattle. Pain seized my joints. I felt like I'd swallowed a wasp and it was trying to sting its way out.

"This is torture," I said. "You can't do this to me."

"Bro, not only am I already doing it to you *as we speak*, but I'm probably gonna get a promotion when all is said and done. Just wait and see. And look at that, Mr. Complainy Pants. You already made a tiny nick. That's progress! I'd say if you do that about 10,000 more times, you might actually start to get somewhere. Higgins? Hey Higgins?"

The lanky guard goosestepped over and saluted the liaison. The liaison lazily saluted him back.

"Higgins, you're on Crumb duty until further notice. Make sure this whiny little bitch keeps working. And if he starts complaining again, you have my permission to shoot him in the dick."

"Roger that, sir."

"Would you stop calling me a whiny little bitch?" I said. But by that point the liaison was already gone.

18.

ALTHOUGH THE FIVE of us trained independently, we still adhered to the same schedule.

We slept in the same barracks at the same hours.

We exercised using the same equipment.

We took all our daily meals in the mess hall at the same time.

The guards and secret servicemen monitored our activity 24/7. They were posted in zigzag patterns throughout the room. Tucked into the corners. By the doors. In the rafters. Everywhere.

Once a day the liaison would pass around the facility and ask if we needed anything. No matter what we requested of him, he'd reply with a chipper "I'll see what I can do!" and then he'd never bring it up again. It was almost like he was telling us what we wanted to hear so we wouldn't complain.

"I'd like to call my wife, please," I asked him once again. Perhaps for the fiftieth time now.

~ SMILE OR ELSE ~ the sign above us said.

I smiled. He smiled back. Just two happy guys having a happy conversation.

"You know contact with the outside world is prohibited, Crumb. It's a matter of national security. For your safety and ours. We couldn't risk any information falling into the wrong hands."

"But whose hands are the wrong hands?" I asked.

39

"Everyone's but ours," he replied.

Every so often the five of us were forced to spend several hours together at one of the small round tables in the kitchen area during non-meal hours for what the liaison called Teamwork Practice.

We weren't given any tasks during this time. In fact, not having any tasks to do was the entire point. In the spaceship we'd be sharing cramped quarters. This was supposed to be a kind of bonding exercise.

We faced each other. Hunkered in close like a cabal of conspirators. Though aside from the general complaints about this whole bullshit situation, none of us ever had any juicy gossip to share. If someone was feeling amicable, they might update the rest of the group on their particular project's progress, but the conversation usually ended there. Nobody offered up any personal details about themselves. Nobody wanted to get close to anyone else. We were coworkers on our best days. Strangers for the rest. They didn't know about Bella. Or Maxine. Or the litany of other little things I had done throughout my life. Any discussion of our time before the Moonfellow Program was either tacit or brief, if it came up at all.

There were usually some guards in the kitchen area, too. A few on duty making sure we were Teamworking properly. The rest at tables nearby. On shift breaks themselves. Off the clock, they'd mostly ignore us, and I got the distinct impression that the majority of them didn't like their jobs any more than we did. But at least they could go home at the end of the day. At least they got to have a life beyond this warehouse. We could hear them from our table, chatting about their families. Their hobbies. Their dumb weekend barbecue plans. Whatever. The occasional bout of laughter would bluster forth. Higgins with his *hyuk-hyuk*. His round little partner with his *bwa-ha-ha*. Some of that deep chest laughter. That I-don't-have-a-care-in-the-world laughter. Only a few hours left 'til quittin' time, they'd say as they got back to work. Pitter-patter, let's get at 'er.

The mood around the Moonfellows table was more akin to high-school detention.

It was Captain Mangrove who often took the initiative during these sessions. He wanted to "rally the troops" as he put it. To boost morale.

"This is your job!" he'd undoubtedly been told. "You're the leader of this mission! So *lead*!"

And Mangrove would've certainly taken such a command to heart. He was the only one of us who came from a military background. He was a man of action. Not a diplomat. Not a science nerd. Certainly not a gravedigger.

"I know this has been difficult," Captain Mangrove addressed the group. "But think about it. We're going to do something important. Something that'll benefit all of humanity. And, beyond that, at the end of the day, we all have each other. We're like the Three Musketeers. Except even better, because there's *five* of us, and that's . . . um . . . uh . . . *three* more . . . ?"

"That's two more, sir," Dr. Chase corrected him.

"*Two* more! See? We got each other's backs already. What a team!"

19.

THE DAYS WERE bleeding into each other like paint on a palette until the afternoon that a sound suddenly filled the warehouse.

I poked my head up out of my practice hole like a prairie dog. I actually managed to get about five feet down into the concrete. And yeah, the liaison was right, it took about 10,000 swings.

"What's that noise?" I asked Higgins, thumbing through a magazine at his post, unconcerned.

"Dunno," he said. "Sounded like some sorta whistle to me."

The liaison scuttled by on the balls of his feet, as if he was too busy to take a full step. He didn't even stop as he told me to dust myself off and line up near the main entrance to the building.

"Come now, Crumb. You too, Higgins. We're getting a visitor. Hurry up! Let's go!"

My body felt like a series of rusty hinges as I made my way across the warehouse.

I silently fell in line with the already-assembled Moonfellows near the entrance.

"What's happening?" I asked Dr. Bhandary.

She shrugged and then *BAM!* the front door to the building swung open as if it were kicked. Sunlight flooded the room like a wave. I hadn't seen the sun in weeks. Seemed brighter than it used to be. Or maybe not. I don't know.

My eyes eventually readjusted and there stood President Harper, plastic smile on his ruggedly handsome face, shoulders almost as broad as the doorway itself.

"Ah, here we are! *Here* we *are*! All my little duckies in a little row!" The President paced back and forth. Heels clicking against the concrete floor like he was wearing tap shoes. "I've been told you've all been keeping busy."

"Yes sir!" Captain Mangrove oorahed. He puffed his chest out like he was expecting to be awarded a medal or something.

"Very good," said the President. "I actually appreciate the gusto. The rest of you could learn a thing or two from your captain here. You're talking to the goddamn Commander-In-Chief. Show some fucking *gusto* fer chrissakes!"

"If they could stick me full of straws and suck the gusto out of me, I would allow it, sir," Mangrove said.

"The rest'a ya hear that?" The President clapped his hands. "That's initiative! That's the kind of dedication we need to ensure success! How many of you sadsacks would be willing to get sucked dry for the good of your country?"

There was a pause in which no one dared breathe, broken only when an unsure Dr. Chase cleared her throat and finally stammered, "I . . . um . . . I guess I am willing to get sucked dry for my country."

"Yeah . . . *erm* . . . me too, sir," Dr. Tanaka chimed in after her.

"And you . . . " President Harper snuck a quick look down, where he jotted the Moonfellows' names on the palm of his hand. " . . . *Dr. Bhandary*. I know there's a part of you that constantly wants to test your mettle. That wants to see what happens when we *really* put that big brain to work. What are you truly capable of, when given free agency and pushed to the absolute limit, huh? I know you'd like to see your name gilded alongside the greats throughout history. Newton. Galileo. Tesla. And perhaps Bhandary someday, too?"

She didn't say a word. Just nodded in the affirmative. Ever so slight.

"Now that's what I'm talking about! Fuck yeah! We're going to take over the fuckin' mooooooooooon!" The President beamed as his gaze then drifted in my direction. He walked over and stood in front of me. Our noses were only inches apart. Appraising me with a wary eye, as if I were an obvious forgery on display in a museum.

He said, "And how about you, Mr. Crumb?"

And I said, "Huh?"

"Do you pledge your unending devotion to me and the Moonfellow Program and the interests of the United States of America? Are you onboard? Are you ready to go?"

"Oh . . . uh . . . " I looked at the rest of the Moonfellows and sighed. "Yeah, sure. I'm with them."

"Wonderful!" President Harper clapped his hands again. "So now that we're all on the same page, I'm happy to report that the five of you will launch tomorrow."

"Tomorrow?!" the suddenly vocal Dr. Bhandary exclaimed. "With all due respect, Mr. President, but what the fuck are you talking about?"

"The mission is to commence tomorrow. Sunrise/sunset. Then you launch. Am I being unclear?"

"Sir, there is still a lot of highly delicate work that needs to be done! We have to be precise. And it takes time to do it right."

President Harper's unctuous smile fell away. He wasn't following his own stupid mandate. He didn't look happy anymore. He barely looked human.

"What did you just say to me?" he said, almost in a growl.

"It's just . . . I'm not going to be ready that soon."

And the President's diplomatic smile returned. As glib as ever.

"Ms. Bhandary, let me ask you a question: do you believe in providence?"

"I'm afraid I don't follow."

"The concept of providence, my dear. The belief that a higher power—be it God or nature or, in your particular case, the President of the United States of America—is guiding and protecting you. A kind of sacred authority, if you will. Bestowed upon a person or group of people. Ordained by the Almighty Himself.

"I'm talking about American Exceptionalism, Dr. Bhandary. Manifest Destiny. Fate. It's all the same thing. The inevitable. The unavoidable. The right to take what God hath given. Providence is the purview of the chosen few. And you and your crew have been chosen because I deemed it so. You *will* be ready by tomorrow, and you *will* go to the moon. Do you understand? Do you all understand?"

Five heads nodded.

Yes.

Yes.

Yes.

Yes.

And Dr. Bhandary let out a heavy breath before shrinking back into line.

Yes.

20.

THERE WERE NO reporters or newscasters present on the day of takeoff.

No spectators beyond a few government officials.

Nobody baked us a 'good luck' cake.

We were the first people in human history to travel beyond the bounds of our humble little planet, and yet, the only fanfare we received was the echo of our own footsteps as we were marched through the facility and into the future.

I spent that morning packing, although I didn't have much to bring. There was my Moonfellow jumpsuit and my government-issued shovel and a couple clean pairs of underwear.

Higgins stood nearby. Service weapon in hand. Waiting to lead me to the launch site.

"Hey Higgins?"

"What is it, Crumb?"

"I got a quick question?"

"Oh no you don't, Crumb. I'mma shut you down before you even begin. You're getting on that damn ship no matter what. Harper told me if anything goes wrong he is gonna literally feed me to alligators. I've seen the tank where he keeps 'em. It's in the basement of the Lincoln Memorial."

"I know. I know," I said. "I'm not trying anything. No funny business, I swear. I just . . . well . . . do you remember where I live?"

"It was like the Sasquatch River or something like that, wasn't it?"

"Sasquahatchee, New Jersey. Yeah."

"Okay, yeah, I remember. But so what?"

"Well, do you think . . . " A single tear rolled down my cheek. I was trying to hold back. But it was little use. "Do you think maybe you can go there and tell Bella something for me?"

"Ah jeez. With the waterworks and everything? Are you friggin' serious right now?"

"Look, I know you can't tell her exactly what's going on here. And I know you can't tell her what really happened to me. But could you at least tell her that I love her? That I did all that I could? Could you tell her that no matter where I go and no matter what happens, she'll always be there, in my thoughts, and in my heart? Could you do that for me, Higgins?"

The guard was so blindsided by this request that he was at a loss for words.

"I don't—"

"Higgins, please," I said. "I'm begging you. *Please*."

He sighed.

"Alright, Crumb. I'll tell her for you. Now grab your shit and c'mon. We're gonna be late."

The five of us were shuffled through a tiny door on the far side of the building. Not the one we'd initially entered, but a second door. A *hidden* door that blended into the wall. Higgins pushed it open. All of us passed through. And for the first time in weeks, we were outside.

It was *hot* and *balmy* and *uncomfortable* out here. A perfectly oppressive summer's day. The surrounding forest seemed so green. Almost too green. Almost psychedelic. It didn't even occur to me then that this might be the last time I ever see a plant. But it was.

Guards were positioned in front of us and behind us. Down a short trail and over the crest of a wooded hill, we marched. Until we came upon a clearing, miles away from civilization. A field shrouded on all sides by verdant hills.

This was where our spaceship was docked. A misshapen Frankenstein of a blimp. An airship so overbuilt and cumbersome it was almost ready to fall apart at the seams.

Attached to the top was a giant, teardrop-shaped balloon constructed out of several hundred aluminum-reinforced silk-polymer patches that had been hastily soldered together earlier that day and inflated to the rupture point with some manner of noble gas.

"It's full of neon," Dr. Bhandary informed us. "It's lighter than air."

"Is this how you intended it to look?" Dr. Tanaka asked.

"I mean, it *sorta* looks like the blueprints I gave them," she said. Next to the launchpad was a pile of junk into which many of the delicate components Dr. Bhandary had spent the past few weeks designing had been tossed. For the sake of efficiency, a few corners were apparently cut. "I was told they had their best technicians on the assembly. It probably just needs a good polish, is all."

The ship powered on and the neon in the dome began to glow. Blades of blinding white light were cast through the cracks in the foil like moonbeams themselves.

"And I suppose it's supposed'ta leak light like that, too, huh?" Dr. Tanaka raised an eyebrow.

"Well how else are you gonna know if it's working?" Dr. Bhandary replied.

As we got closer, I could see that the craft was already hovering a few feet in the air. A dozen or so secret servicemen kept it tethered to the ground with a network of ropes. It was kind of like a float at the Thanksgiving Day Parade. A giant Hersey's kiss.

The bulk of the cabin was built out of a repurposed old train car. I recognized it almost immediately. It was the train that derailed into the Sasquahatchee River a few weeks ago. I had buried most of the bodies from this accident. Bloodstains still covered the side of it. Gory desperate fingerprints freckled the bottom like barnacles.

The cabin, cockpit, and boosters all hung from the balloon by a trellis of thin girders, with Dr. Tanaka's mirrored sat-e-lite ball tied underneath like a potbelly. There was a release valve located inside the craft somewhere for easy deployment of it once we were in space.

Across the side of the vessel the name had been painted. Sloppy bold letters. Like it'd been scrawled by a child.

SELENE ONE

Our home away from home away from home.

I figured 'SELENE' was just another made-up nonsense word like Moonfellow but Dr. Tanaka later told me that in Greek mythology, Selene is the goddess of the Moon.

"What makes her so special?" I asked him.

"She drove her chariot across Heaven," he said. "And she fucked Zeus."

"But doesn't Zeus fuck everybody?"

"Yeah, dude. He was the man."

21.

IF THIS WHOLE thing seems anticlimactic that's because it was.

The President kept commenting how this was a "momentous occasion" but with no press corps or witnesses or even our families on-site, it felt more like a lackluster garden party than the launch of the world's first interstellar airship.

A podium had been set up. President Harper stood behind it. The five of us were lined up on the dais behind him. There were only a few assorted G-men in attendance. Most of them seemed bored. Higgins even had his eyes closed. I was pretty sure he fell asleep.

"Welp, here they are, folks," the President said. "The Moonfellows. Aren't they cute? Yeah, they're alright.

"So this is it, everybody. The end of a long and tumultuous road. Behind you are all the painfully unexceptional days of your life as you once lived them. Ahead of you is tomorrow and all the possibility it brings. You were once a buncha nobodies. You were nothing. But I changed all that. I made you special. You should be thanking me. You should be genuflecting at my feet. You should be lining up to kiss my pinky ring. And if we had time, I would make you do just that.

"And you may be asking yourself now—as humankind has done in the past when faced with any new and uncertain endeavor—why? Why go to the moon? Why set such lofty goals? Why do men climb the highest mountains? Why must we eat all our vegetables first if we want dessert?

"Well, we *choose* to go to the moon, as we *choose* to do all those other things too, and we *choose* these paths not because they are easy, but because they are hard. I swear, y'all have been the biggest bunch of bellyachers I've ever met in my life. I am giving you a wonderful gift. If this were Russia, I would've had you all beheaded two weeks ago for insubordination. They do that over there, ya know. No trial or anything. You look at the Russian President the wrong way and *thwack!* heads are rolling like apples down the streets of Saint Petersburg. But alas, America is a *civilized* nation and we have to adhere to 'due process'—whatever the hell that means. My point is, I think we have a lot we could learn from our Siberian brothers and sisters. At the very least it'd make you think twice before giving me guff. Hey, can someone refresh my drink? You. You there, waiter. Look, I know you're not a real waiter, but you're standing near me: can you go fetch me another high ball? Thanks, bud. Anyway, where was I? I forgot. Well whatever. Sayonara, suckerssssss!"

22.

THE DOOR TO the capsule squealed on its hinges as it slid shut behind us. Something clunked towards the rear of the ship. Something else clunked towards the front.

The interior was dark. The air felt stale.

Although there were portholes along either side, they were small and almost swallowed up by a large *computation machine* that took up at least a third of the living space. A *cal-cu-lay-tor*, is what I heard someone call it, and apparently, it could do math super fast. Addition and subtraction only, Dr. Bhandary later told me. And only whole numbers. We hadn't the technology for fractions yet. And it would take a cal-cu-lay-tor the size of Rhode Island if you wanted to do long division.

A cramped kitchenette sat in the middle of the chamber. A hotplate and a water dispenser and about a month's worth of food were stored in cabinets beneath the two-seater table. Also in storage was my shovel, along with Bethany's microscopes, and the monitor/receiver part of Kenji Tanaka's sat-e-lite telecaster.

In the back part of the ship were the sleeping quarters. Our cots were lined up around the perimeter of the tube so that we all faced inward toward each other. BDSM-style harnesses would keep us from floating out of bed while in zero gravity. The nipple clamps, we were told, were for our own protection.

Behind a see-through lace curtain lay the bathroom

stall. There was no shower or place to wash up. The toilet was this diaper-like apparatus you slid your legs into before throwing a nearby switch. A vacuum would literally suck the waste right out of your body. *Slurp*. Like a hungry mosquito. It was very efficient, and physically-speaking, not an altogether unpleasant experience.

I took my seat with the other Moonfellows in the cockpit. Captain Mangrove sat at the helm. Dr. Bhandary in the chair next to him. The co-pilot. I was toward the back. Behind everyone else. Like the luggage. There were dozens of switches and levers and buttons all around me, some blinking like fireflies, others spinning like pinwheels. It was actually surprisingly similar to the Captain's old practice bathtub.

I didn't touch anything. I was too afraid. I strapped myself in and checked the seatbelt, over and over again, tightening it a little bit more with every pass.

I could barely breathe as Mangrove ran through his "pre-flight checklist" (I think that's what he called it, he was using a lot of technical jargon) and then flipped a lever. The whole ship rattled as the balloon on top began to respire. Sucking air in and out. *Crinkle-crinkle*. Like robot lungs.

The sound of creaking metal settling into place as the whole contraption hovered. No more than a few feet. The final countdown commenced:

—5—
—4—
—3—
—2—
—1—

The government agents let go of the ropes.
The President saluted us *bon voyage*!
And we floated away.

23.

Higher we went. And for the moment, things were deceptively calm.

Outside the window, everything around us got smaller. There was the warehouse. Shrinking to the size of a dollhouse. A matchbook. A postage stamp. A pinprick. When we were inside, it seemed impossibly large, but from this height you'd never know it was down there at all.

Washington DC soon followed suit. The bustling metropolis looked like an anthill on the side of the Earth. Even higher, and I could see the ocean. The swirling patterns in the storm clouds over the seaboard. My home state of New Jersey just an indistinguishable smear of brown and green, no more defined than any of the other landmasses below. Bella must be down there. Somewhere. At that very moment. Maybe she was washing the dishes. Maybe she was reading a book. Maybe she was taking a walk through the Lone Fir Cemetery without me. I was headed in the wrong direction. Toward the stupid fucking moon.

The blue sky gave way to black as we floated into the thermosphere.

"Elevation?" Captain Mangrove asked Dr. Bhandary.

"100,000 kilometers," she replied, reading the number off the gauge.

"Did you say kilometers?"

" . . . yeah?"

"Did we not get these instruments converted to Imperial?"

"I guess not."

"So how high is that in feet then?"

"How the hell should I know?"

He looked out the window—first to the Earth, then up at the stars.

"Meh, this seems high enough to me," Mangrove said. "Prepare to disengage."

There was a click as the girders that held the fuselage and the balloon together uncoupled. The balloon was instantly taken by a zephyr and whisked away.

"Ohshitohshitohshitohshit," I gasped as gravity asserted itself upon the clunky cabin. The cockpit tipped downward. We were plummeting full-speed back towards the ground.

G-forces slammed my head against the chair and contorted my face like clay. The same was happening to everyone else. Dr. Tanaka was twisted up like a Picasso painting, eyes and nose and mouth akimbo. Dr. Chase and Dr. Bhandary looked like ice sculptures melting in the sun. My fingers dug into my armrests so hard that my knuckles turned white.

Of course, Captain Mangrove wasn't fazed by any of this. He actually looked like he was having fun. An almost sociopathic smile crept across his face while the rest of us screamed in mortal terror.

"Thrusters?" he said to Dr. Bhandary.

"What?" she eked out.

"What is the status of the thrusters?"

"Online! They're online! Fuckin' hell, Dirk, we're gonna die!"

"Yeah? Well lemme see if I can just crank these sonofabitches up and fix that. Get ready, nerds. Escape velocity, here we come!"

The boosters kicked on. Captain Mangrove strained as

he pulled back on the yoke with all his might. Muscles in his neck stuck out like harp strings.

"C'mon! C'mon, you bitch! C'mon!"

We leveled out and our trajectory turned from the Earth to the clouds. No longer in a nosedive, but rocketing forward, leaving a contrail of smoke and fire across the firmament. A runaway train streaking across the sky.

"There we go," he said, as he pulled back on the yoke further, asserting even more control over the vessel. The front of the SELENE ONE now tilted upward. Into space. Our tiny blue planet receded like the tide as we headed into orbit.

"Easy as pie," Captain Mangrove said. "I didn't doubt myself for a second."

24.

OUR SPACE SHUTTLE puttered like a fishing trawler across the stars. We were somewhere in the middle of our three-day journey between the Earth and the moon. Our home planet looked so small. Like nothing at all. A dollop of green paint against a black canvas.

One night I found myself awake while the rest of the crew slept around me. Strapped to their cots in the bedchamber in the rear of the vessel.

I was having a difficult time adjusting to my newfound weightlessness. My insides were unmoored. Sloshing around beneath my skin. Making me nauseous. I couldn't shake it. I didn't feel like I was floating. I felt like I was falling. Like I'd suddenly been pushed off the side of a cliff. Endlessly falling, without ever hitting the ground.

The lights were switched to night mode. A calming ocean blue. The ship was quiet save for the cacophonous clatter of its inner machinery at work.

I unhooked myself and made my way to the main quarters to fix myself some chamomile. There I found Dr. Bhandary already awake as well. She must have snuck by me. I hadn't even heard her get up. She was looking out of a porthole at our home planet below.

She acknowledged me with a cursory glance. Without saying a word, I filled two tea pouches up with hot water and handed one to her. I slid up to the adjacent porthole and looked out as well.

"Can't sleep?" I said.

She shook her head no.

"Yeah, me neither."

We looked at the little Earth for a while longer.

"It's kinda beautiful, though, isn't it?" I said.

"Probably more beautiful from up here than it is from down there," she conceded.

"Kinda freaky to think we're the first people to ever see the Earth from this distance. Lotta philosophers have come and gone throughout history. Everyone is trying to figure out what it means to be human. Yet none of them ever got to glimpse at the big picture."

"So you got anything philosophical to say about it then?"

"Not really. No."

We lapsed back into silence. Sipping our tea to the sounds of Mangrove snoring in the back.

"You know, I only took the job at the Lone Fir because I needed the work and they happened to be hiring. I saw the want ad in the newspaper. And I thought, why not? I'd never dug a hole in my life before then. I was just filling out applications. Whatever was available. There were a million other professions in the world. I could've ended up a florist. Or a carpenter. Or cleaning up piles of elephant shit at the circus. The last thing the moon needed was a fucking florist, right?"

"We don't get to rewrite the past, Crumb. You tip the dominoes in a different direction and everything changes. Think of all that has happened since then. Think of what you'd stand to lose."

Yeah. These are dangerous thoughts. We have to suffer for the things that matter. For Bella. For Maxine. For the life I once had. Would I sacrifice it all to spare myself the pain of having it taken away?

Bella and I met at the Lone Fir. I spotted her from across the cemetery. Like an orchid against the colorless landscape. As gentle and graceful as the rolling fog.

I was in a half-finished grave. Dirt up to my elbows like I was bathing in it. Our eyes met. I smiled at her. She smiled back. That was all it took. Sometimes you just know.

Our first date was a picnic. At midnight. In this same graveyard. The place where we met. Perhaps it was a bit morbid. A cemetery at night. But there was something sort of magical about it, too. I wanted to share it with her. I wanted her to see what I saw. That even the darkest places sometimes held a hidden kind of beauty.

She wore a floral print sundress and straw bonnet. She was dressed like we were on our way to church. I had on a blazer and borrowed a tie. I must have looked like a schoolboy who had wandered down the wrong trail in the woods.

People used to say the moonlight was romantic. They wrote songs about it. And there the moon sat, so plump and pale and full of promise. Casting the world around us in shades of blue.

We ate cheese and fruit and drank a little wine and I took her on a quick tour of the grounds, pointing out all the tombstones that I thought were funny.

Here Lies
Harold Dicker

Fannie Pancakes
Beloved Wife and Mother

Rest in Peace
Mr. Jackson Cornelius Fartwiener IV

As I repeated the names to Dr. Bhandary, she couldn't help but chuckle aloud, the same as Bella once did, all those years ago. I suppose the name 'Fannie Pancakes' will never not be hilarious.

"And what about you, doc?" I asked. "Did you hafta leave anyone behind?"

Her smile faded and she tucked a wild curl of dark hair behind her ear, a delicate yet purposeful movement, as if she was knitting a quilt.

"I sacrificed a lot to get here, Crumb. In a lot of ways, I didn't even know this was where I was headed. But I don't look backward. I don't have any regrets. I was alone before the Moonfellows began. And I'll be alone again long after the Moonfellows are gone."

I nodded. As if I understood.

And the outboard motor puttered us farther and farther from home.

25.

THE SAFE-LITE DEPLOYMENT went off without incident. At the time, I thought it boded well.

Dr. Tanaka pulled the ripcord and the device disengaged with a *chonk*. I looked out the window. Saw it floating in the space behind us like it was suspended in Jell-O. Sunlight bounced off the reflective panels—a man-made shooting star. Halfway between here and there. Just a twinkle. Just a speck. Just a lonely disco ball above an empty dance floor.

Then came the moon.

No longer a dot in the sky but a planet unto its own.

It loomed on the horizon like a giant golf ball. Valleys and craters and ridges of dusty rock stretched endlessly across its pallid surface. As surreal as we ever imagined it. A celestial desert, unreachable to humankind for millennia. For all of human history. Until now.

"It's beautiful," said Dr. Chase, her voice barely more than a whisper.

Captain Dirk Mangrove sat in the pilot's seat, checking the nozzles and switches and other assorted doodaddery.

"Preparing the ship for landing," he said.

And then:

Something went wrong.

Some unknown piece fell out of place.

Perhaps it began with a single screw. We'll never know. And I suppose it doesn't matter, anyway.

Several systems failed in rapid succession. It was a cascading effect. One problem after another. So quickly it was impossible to pinpoint what the catalyst was.

The steering yoke suddenly locked up.

The wiring short-circuited.

Sparks like fireworks filled my vision.

"What's happening?!" screamed Dr. Tanaka.

"I don't know!" Captain Mangrove replied. "The control panel is unresponsive! I think the fuel tank ruptured! The entire ship is falling apart!"

One of the sides of the capsule crumpled like a kicked-in tin can. The cabin immediately depressurized. The air was sucked out of my lungs so quickly I couldn't even gasp for it. My blood boiled and leaked out of my nose. Fear paralyzed me. I couldn't move. I couldn't do anything at all.

We careened out of control. Fires broke out everywhere. The SELENE ONE tumbled end over end as we plunged through the lunar atmosphere. The ground rapidly approached. Everything unraveled. I thought of Bella. I thought of Maxine. My unexceptional life. Everything that was stolen from me.

The ship split in half and the silence of space rushed in behind it. A nothingness so oppressive it was as if God himself were holding his hands over our screaming mouths.

We slammed into the moon. And it all went black.

26.

I DON'T KNOW how long I was out. Days. Years. Decades. In the darkness, all time is the same.

One by one, we climbed out of the wreckage. Battered and bruised and shaken up like soda cans. It was a miracle no one was dead. Yet.

When I finally opened my eyes, the first thing I saw was Mangrove planting an American flag into the soil in front of me.

"One small step for man," he said. "One big-ass explosion for mankind. That was fuckin' crazy. Now get up, Crumb. Naptime is over and no one is paying you to sleep while the rest of us gotta work."

We inspected the damage. It was as if something had clawed the ship in half. Both alloy and aluminum torn as easily as cheesecloth. A complete assessment had to be done before any sort of status report could be given. Dr. Bhandary surveyed the crash site and collected the debris.

"This is an unmitigated disaster," was her official conclusion. In the flight log she took a black marker and scrawled the words W-E A-R-E F-U-C-K-E-D.

"But what is the actual scope of the damage?" asked Dr. Chase.

"You have eyes—don't you, Dr. Chase? The scope of the damage is exhaustive and complete. This is the kind of situation that we engineers refer to as *FUBAR*."

Dr. Chase slumped over. Dr. Tanaka let out a defeated

sigh. Off to the side, Captain Mangrove was talking to the moon slug he held in his hand.

"I'm gonna name you Bilbo Sluggins," he said, as he petted the top of its head. He didn't seem too concerned about our current predicament. He'd been delighted by the slugs since we found them, almost immediately upon exiting the crash.

"Well, I hope you're happy," Dr. Bhandary said, as she stormed toward him.

"What?" said Mangrove.

She slapped the tiny gastropod out of his hand. It hit the dirt and ceased moving.

"What the hell, you asshole? That was Bilbo Sluggins!"

"I don't give a fuck!"

She lunged at him. The rest of us swooped in. Dr. Chase restrained Dr. Bhandary. Dr. Tanaka did the same with the Captain.

"You destroyed the fucking ship, you moron," Dr. Bhandary shouted at him. "It's literally in a thousand pieces! It's an unfixable mess!"

"You think this is my fault?" Captain Mangrove shouted back. "You're the one who designed the stupid thing. That's your shoddy craftsmanship scattered across the moon. You wanna scream at me, toots? I managed to somehow set that flaming turd down without killing us all."

"Call me *toots* again and I'll cut your dick off."

"You ain't got a pair of scissors strong enough."

"Cool it, you two," I weakly said. I stood between them with my arms out. An ineffectual referee.

Mangrove broke free from Dr. Tanaka's grasp.

"Fuck you, too, you fuckin' *gravedigger*," he said. "You ghoulish fuck. What are you even doing up here, anyway? Could we have not just brought a backhoe or something? I'm the goddamn *Captain*. I killed twenty-seven men during the Spanish-American War. You think I hafta put up with your bullshit? I landed this hunk of crap. I'm the reason any of us are still breathing."

He turned and stomped off. Away from the four of us. Through the dust and the soil and the slugs. Heading nowhere in particular. Everywhere was nowhere on the moon.

"You can't fly for shit," Dr. Bhandary yelled after him. "You ruined my ship."

"Let him go," Dr. Chase said, as Mangrove disappeared over the cusp of a nearby ridge, muttering and cursing to himself as he went.

Dr. Tanaka took this opportunity to address the rest of us. The cut across his forehead was already clotted. It would definitely make a cool scar one day, unlike the cut across my forehead, which was shaped like a tiny penis. I would have a tiny penis-shaped scar on my face for the rest of my life.

"Alright look, I'll be the first to admit it. Things are bad. But they're not hopeless just yet. We got the sat-e-lite into orbit, right? It was probably the only part of this mission that went off without a hitch, eh? Not to toot my own horn or anything. No offense, Kari. My point is, we can use the telecaster to call back to Earth. Let 'em know what happened. Let 'em know we're alive. They'll send out a rescue mission to come get us. And everything will be okay."

"Slight problem, Kenji . . . " Dr. Chase pointed at a pile of rubble. The telecaster lay there in the middle of it. Dented up. Sparking. Wires like intestines spilling out of its side.

Dr. Tanaka's face instantly dropped.

"Oh goddamn it."

27.

OUR FIRST NIGHT on the moon. In the shade of the Earth. Shadows like spilled motor oil stretched across the horizon. The back half of the ship lay partially intact. Our home base. Our sleeping quarters. And the power stayed on thanks to a bit of creative rewiring from Dr. Tanaka and Dr. Bhandary.

They worked together. Discarding fuses. Rerouting currents. Wrapping wires and cables around the SELENE ONE so curly and thick it looked like pubic hair.

Battery terminals were plugged back into themselves— a feedback loop able to sustain a charge just strong enough to keep the lights on and the heat running indefinitely.

"Is this safe?" I asked. "This thing looks like a bomb."

"I wouldn't worry too much about it, Crumb,' Dr. Bhandary said. "I mean, sure, we might explode at any moment, but at least we won't freeze to death."

As the sun set, Captain Mangrove still hadn't returned, though just past midnight, I could've sworn I'd heard him. A voice in the distance. Coming up with names for more of the slugs.

"Swimple Swimon."

"Princess Boogerbeans."

"Robert Snailford."

"Robert Snailford Jr."

"Robert Snailford III."

And so on.

MOONFELLOWS

And when morning rolled around, we got back to work.

Dr. Tanaka swore he'd be able to get the sat-e-lite telecast functional again. I wanted to believe him, but I couldn't see how. The side was cracked open and various bits of the circuitry were scattered about. He was taking inventory. Seeing what he had. And what he could do.

"Luckily, the most important components remained intact," he said. The tele-vision screen suffered only a hairline crack and the antenna on top was bent but not broken. "Might take a while, but I should be able to jury-rig it back together. Wish I had some glue, though."

"I might actually be able to help you with that," Dr. Chase said. She'd already set up her salvaged lab equipment outside the SELENE ONE. Soil samples. Slug samples. The tiny MacGuffinite sample we'd brought with us from Earth. She was running experiments. Making observations. Doing what she could with what little furnishings she had.

She dusted off a shard of broken curved metal and used it to scrape the underbelly of one of the moon slugs. Slime collected in the ladle, as thick as pea soup. She handed it over to Dr. Tanaka, who smeared it on the side of the telecaster and stuck some loose scrap to it, sealing the crack.

"Great!" he chirped. "A natural adhesive."

"Yeah. They're a bit stickier than the leopard slugs from back home. A bit *sluggier,* too, if that makes sense. I'm not quite sure what the deal is yet. But we'll figure it out. It's not like there's any shortage of test subjects."

Endless waves of gastropods squirmed toward us. A sea of slugs. Perhaps drawn to the ship, the warmth of the thrumming battery, the color, the noise, the bevy of scientists all in a furor. Perhaps they were curious. Perhaps they were slug scientists themselves. Or perhaps they saw us as their ticket out of here. Who could say?

28.

MY FIRST EXCAVATION.

My second excavation.
My third.
Fourth.
And fifth.

I would turn the moon to Swiss cheese if I had to. I would not quit until I held a big ole chunk of MacGuffinite in my hand. Dr. Chase told me it might be toxic. But I didn't care. Confirm. Extract. Return. That was the mission. MacGuffinite was the lynchpin to this whole operation. The fulcrum around which everything pivoted. If we found the MacGuffinite, we would find a way off the moon. It was hope. It was salvation. It was survival. It was everything.

My holes were six feet in diameter. Fifteen feet deep. And set twenty yards apart in a sort of nautilus-like pattern starting at the crash site and spiraling out from there, methodically upending the moon behind me. The soil was soft. I could work very quickly. There was no patch of land that went unchecked. I was a bulldozer. A human steam shovel.

I dug fifty holes before lunch. And by dinnertime, I dug fifty more.

It was late afternoon and I was out on the range, the SELENE ONE a speck in the distance, finishing the last few digs of the day, when a deep muffled voice suddenly called out my name.

68

"Crumb . . . "

I shot up. Stared at the ground. It sounded like the voice was coming from beneath me. But that was impossible. Was there someone . . . underneath the dirt . . . ?

"It's just the acoustics, dummy. I'm up here."

I looked up. Standing on the lip of the hole I was in was Mangrove, his wide chest eclipsing the meager sun. I was engulfed by his shadow.

"Captain Mangrove?" I said. "Is that you?"

"Yeah, it's me, Crumb. Your fearless leader."

"It's been, like, three days since anyone's seen you, sir."

"What are you, an hourglass? I can tell time, Crumb."

"Where the hell did you go?"

"Nowhere. I was just over there. Around the corner. Don't worry about it."

"What?"

"Look, I don't need a goddamn inquisition, okay? Especially not from a subordinate like you. Now climb on out of that stupid hole. I need to tell you something important. Lemme help."

He reached down and our hands clasped together.

His palm was warm and clammy, like he was running hot with fever. I used his strength to help hoist myself out of the dig site. He didn't even grunt as he lifted me up. But there was something off about him. Some undefinable thing. He had the same broad stance. The same pearly white teeth. The same boxy chin. No, it was his eyes. His eyes looked different. Like they were set just slightly too far apart. Like they had slowly begun to drift away. I couldn't quite explain it. The same with his skin, now a slightly different color too. Once a healthy shade of brown, it now appeared somewhat sallow. Almost as if he were covered in a giant bruise.

We didn't know about the Moon Flu yet. We didn't know he'd already been infected. Looking back now, it was obvious. His sclerae were bloodshot and his nose was running. A trail of clear mucus shimmered on his upper lip. He kept licking it clean.

I was dusting myself off when Mangrove suddenly gripped me by the shoulders. His demeanor changed. His body shook. His eyes widened. An insane twinkle swirled within them. Our noses were only a few inches apart.

"I know you're doing your best, Crumb, but you're wasting your time. You might as well dig a hole and stay down there yourself. You're never going to find anything under the dirt."

His fingers pressed into my shoulder meat. I tried to wiggle loose but could not.

"Wha—what?"

"It's just the way it is, Crumb. It's written in the stars, if you will. There is no MacGuffinite. There are no answers buried beneath our feet. There is nothing on the moon. There never was."

"Dirk?" the distant voice of Dr. Tanaka yelled out. "Dirk? Captain Mangrove, is that you?"

The electronics expert came running toward us. The rest of the Moonfellows followed closely behind. Mangrove let go of my shoulders and turned toward his crew with his hands in the air.

"Hey gang. No worries. I just bumped into Crumb. He's doing a fantastic job out here. In fact, you all are. I know things were kinda tense when we first landed, but that's yesterday's news. I want us to work together. Now, c'mon. I want to introduce you to all my *other* new friends. This is Robert Snailford, and Robert Snailford Jr., and Robert Snailford III, and Robert Snailford IV . . . "

29.

"MAYBE WE SHOULD start eating the slugs."

The thought must have already crossed a few other minds. But I was the first one to say it out loud. Almost a month on the moon and provisions were running low. Right now we had another two days of food and water. Tops. And we were still no closer to rescue than when we first crashed. I wasn't quite ready to start cannibalizing my crewmates just yet. Eating the slugs seemed to be our only logical alternative.

"I mean, I'm sure they won't taste very good. And they're certainly not gonna digest well, either. But they're probably still edible. Or at least edible-*ish*. People eat snails in France, don't they? There's gotta be some nutritional value to them."

"The question isn't as to their nutritional value," Dr. Bhandary said. "The question is whether or not they're safe to consume at all."

We looked to Dr. Chase for an answer. The geologist cleared her throat and adjusted her glasses but could only offer us a noncommittal shrug.

"Well I suppose 'safe' would be kind of a relative term here. You have to understand this is not my area of expertise. I'm still learning quite a bit about these things myself. But a week or so back I was running a few experiments, and during one of the dissections I noticed something peculiar."

"What?" I said.

"That glow. That unmistakable glow. It was MacGuffinite, woven around their RNA like an incandescent thread. I'm talking just the teeniest of observable amounts. Not enough to measure. Certainly not enough to extract. I've studied the soil here pretty extensively, and though I haven't found any evidence of MacGuffinite in it, I think these slugs are able to absorb the *essence* of it through the moon dust somehow. Traces of MacGuffinite are fortifying these slugs. Like a suit of armor reinforcing their genes. I believe this is how they've adapted to survive on the lunar surface. And how they've proliferated in such massive numbers since."

"Makes them extra gluey, too," Dr. Tanaka chimed in. "I've been milking these little fuckers all over my telecaster. Using 'em to seal up everything nice and tight. Really does the trick."

Dr. Bhandary shook her head. "I'm sorry, what exactly are you telling us, Beth? That there is MacGuffinite *inside* these things?"

"In soluble amounts. Yes. There is," Dr. Chase replied. "But think of it kinda like the iron in your blood. You don't walk around clanking like a set of rusty old chains, do you? Iron is an immutable part of you, just as MacGuffinite appears to be an immutable part of them."

"Okay, but where did it come from?" I asked.

"The iron in your blood?" she replied.

"No, the fuckin' MacGuffinite. Jeezus."

"Aren't you the one who should be telling me that, Franklin?" Dr. Chase volleyed back. "That is your job, is it not? Maybe you're just not looking hard enough."

"I thought you said this MacGuffinite shit is toxic," Dr. Bhandary said. "How are the slugs not affected by it then?"

"They might very well be affected by it, Dr. Bhandary. MacGuffinite is what we call an *endocrine disruptor*. Even in these innumerably small amounts, the potential for serious side effects is there. I'm talking renal failure. Cirrhosis. Cancer. Dementia. Not to mention the whole host of unknown and rampant anatomical mutations that may occur. It's completely unpredictable, suffice it to say, this stuff'll really fuck you up if you let it."

"So we're gonna starve to death, after all?"

"Perhaps," said Dr. Chase. "But then again, perhaps not. What I've recently discovered but have yet to test is that if we're able to introduce these slugs to a high enough heat source, we might be able to negate the more egregious effects of the trace MacGuffinite on the human lymphatic system."

I nodded. "Okay, but what does the word *lymphatic* mean? Also, what do the words *egregious* and *negated* mean as well?"

"What I'm saying is, if you were to throw a couple of 'em on that hotplate there in the SELENE ONE and boil them down into this here sludge . . . " She held up a vial of melted slug. It was the color of shit and smelled just about as appetizing. "It should cook the toxins right out of 'em. They're kinda like rhubarb in that way. There is no reason why these slugs shouldn't be able to supply us with a small but sustainable amount of sustenance for the duration of our stay. I believe this test tube of slime is pretty much all we'd need to survive on the moon indefinitely."

"Oh puh-leaze!" Captain Dirk Mangrove scoffed, his limbs swollen, his head sinking into his neck, beads of oily sweat leaking out of his brow, eyes poking nearly an inch out of his skull. "Who's got time for all that rigmarole? I've been eatin' these li'l boogers raw since the day we got here and I've never felt better in my whole damn life!"

30.

IT SOON BECAME apparent that it wasn't just the physical appearance of Captain Mangrove that was off. Yes, his old teeth were falling out and a set of new fang-like teeth were growing in, but that could've been for any number of reasons. Maybe it was simply a bad case of gingivitis. The problem was that there were other increasingly-strange behaviors he was exhibiting, as well. The Moon Flu was avalanching through his system. Metastasizing inside his DNA. Or RNA. Or NRA. Or whatever it was called. He was rapidly transforming into something else. Something new. Something none of us had ever seen before. Something none of us quite understood.

There were times when I would catch him staring off at nothing. The five of us Moonfellows would be having a group discussion. Hashing out our next steps and divvying out the responsibilities. Mangrove would slowly fade from the conversation. His pupils would grow and his eyes would glaze over. It was as if all the thoughts suddenly fell out of his head. He wouldn't even blink. It was like he forgot how. And if we questioned him about it, he'd act affronted.

"What do you mean 'am I okay?' Do I not seem okay to you? If anything, you're the ones who need help. Not me. Stop wasting my time with these stupid questions. Now everybody drop and give me twenty. I'm gonna go take a nap."

MOONFELLOWS

The way his body moved changed, too. It was as if he were losing control of it. He'd always been a large man with a large stride. He had heavy feet that clomped against the moon's surface like the hooves of a Clydesdale. But now he walked with a distinct shuffle. His feet stayed on the ground. He dragged himself through the dust. He moved almost silently. Slithering on by.

One restless night I looked over to find his bunk empty.

The rest of the Moonfellows were asleep, Dr. Bhandary and Dr. Chase and Dr. Tanaka, strapped into their cots for the evening. Snoring. Dreaming. But the blankets on Mangrove's bed had been ruffled and kicked off. His pillows lay on the floor. And he was gone.

I ran my fingers along his mattress. It was covered in some sort of . . . *viscous fluid*. Foul-smelling. Gummy and thick. Sweat, I figured. Or perhaps saliva. Or mayonnaise.

I exited the fuselage. The moon at night was even quieter than it was in the day. Everything looked pale. Like the skin of a cadaver.

And I found Captain Mangrove. Not too far away.

He was naked. Lying on his belly. Slugs surrounded him like he was making snow angels. Some watching the proceedings. Some participating as well.

Mangrove caressed the dust beneath him like it were the body of a lover, his bare pelvis moving, up and down, up and down, in and out, in and out—a soft yet satisfied moan rattled around in his chest, his leathery buttchecks clenching tighter with every new thrust.

I looked away. This was not meant for my eyes.

Captain Dirk Mangrove was having sex with the moon.

31.

MANGROVE INSISTED ON joining me on my dig the next day.

He said he wanted to get a lay of the land.

"There's not much land to get a lay of," I assured him. "It's mostly all the same."

But he wasn't buying it. He had his own ideas of how things should go.

"When Lewis and Clark were forging their way along the Oregon Trail, they weren't *just* lookin' for the Pacific. There was an entire country for them to discover, between here and there. They had to catalog every hill. They had to name every river. The two of 'em literally put America onto the map. Kinda like the two of us, Crumb."

"So what's the plan then?" I asked, as I climbed out of the hole I'd just dug. No MacGuffinite down there either. "You wanna create a map of the moon or something?"

"The moon?" he said, with a crooked smile. "Oh, you mean Planet Mangrove?"

We worked our way westward. Toward the once distant ridge bifurcating the horizon, raised from the moonscape like a scar, a forty-foot dust dune that seemed to split the day in two. One half bathed in sunlight. The other half forever shrouded by night. The dark side of the moon lay on the other side. It was like a curtain drawn across the sky.

I dug another hole. Nothing. Another hole. Again nothing. Still spiraling away from our base camp. Captain

Mangrove excreted petroleum jelly-thick globs of milky slime from out his pores. *Plop. Plop. Plop. Plop.* Like a trail of breadcrumbs behind him.

And we came upon a massive crater. A giant hole in the ground. Deeper than I could ever dig. Deeper than any hole I'd ever seen before.

"Wouldja lookit this . . . " Mangrove said. His buggy eyes protruded from his face like golf tees, moving independently of each other, looking in two different directions at the same time.

"It's huge," I concurred. "Like an ocean or something. I bet it was caused by one of those *cratering events* Dr. Chase was talking about. From an asteroid or whatever. She said something like this sent the MacGuffinite out into space in the first place. It woulda been shot through the cosmos before falling to the Earth. Crazy, right? I mean, what are the chances? It all seems so implausible."

Mangrove peered over the edge and shook his head.

"Nice theory, but I don't see any MacGuffinite down there either, Crumb."

I also peered over the edge. It didn't even appear to have a bottom. A few slugs slithered around the rim of it until the darkness swallowed them up. What hope did my little shovel and I have?

"Hey Crumb, can I ask you a question?"

I turned to the Captain. His head looked like it had doubled in size and collapsed into his shoulders within the last few minutes. His arms and legs were shorter and fatter, too. He didn't look like he could even lift them anymore. It was like he was slowly disappearing into his swollen torso. Body nothing more than one big tumor on the verge of rupture. Mangrove had been ravaged by the Moon Flu. The disease wasn't going to slow down. He was running out of time.

"Yeah. Okay. What is it?"

"What do you think happens when you die?"

"Uhh . . . what?"

"The afterlife," he said. "Whadaya think comes next?"

"Why are you asking me this, sir?"

"I dunno, Crumb. Just been on my mind, I guess. You used to be a gravedigger, didn'tcha? I suspect you've seen a lotta funerals. Met a lotta grieving people. Encountered a lotta loss. I'm sure you've watched the preachers come in and give their little pep talks to everyone. Comfortin' folks with images of Heaven and salvation and all that hullabaloo. I never thought much about death before I became a Moonfellow. Now it's all I can think about. I was wonderin' if you had any insight for me."

"Well, if I had to guess, I'd say that nothing comes next."

"Nothing?"

"Yeah. Nothing. I don't believe in an afterlife. I don't think anything happens when you die. You just disappear. In an instant. *Pow*. It all goes away. A chasm of nothingness so empty that you're not even aware there is a chasm at all. You're unmade. Like how it was before you were born."

"You just disappear?"

"Yeah. Ashes to ashes. Dust to dust. Don't they say that in the Bible? It's gotta certain kind of symmetry to it. Poetic in a way. Like a perfectly balanced equation. Or an evening of the scales."

Captain Mangrove made a face like he'd just been force-fed a lemon.

"Nah, man. Fuck that. Fuck symmetry. And fuck poetry, too. That's a boring explanation. I thought you were better than that, Crumb. I wanted something to chew on. I wanted philosophy. I wanted profundity. There's nothing revolutionary about nothingness. That's a cop-out answer."

I shrugged. I've sat through a lot of funeral services at the Lone Fir. None of them have ever helped me.

"So you know what I think happens when you die?" Mangrove asked.

"What?" I replied.

"I think there is a Heaven. And I think it's a lot like outer space."

"Oh yeah?"

"Yeah. I think Heaven will look just like the moon. With a real thin atmosphere so everything is bouncy, and all the people will be able to just float around and hang out like they were nothing more than half-inflated balloons. It'll be real fun. All your friends and family will be there. And you could reach into the ground and pull out whatever you wanted. A birthday cake. A rocket ship. A million dollars in diamonds. Whatever you could imagine. It'll be right there, in the dirt. You could plant trees if you wanted. You could rearrange it so that it looked exactly like Earth. There is no nothingness. And there is no god to judge you either. Nothing ever has to change. You never have to change. And it just keeps going on like that. Forever and ever."

At first, I almost laughed. But the more I thought about it, the sadder I became.

"Actually, you know what, sir? I hope you're right."

32.

"IT'S FIXED. Holy shit. I've done it."

Dr. Tanaka came scooting over, hands up with open palms, eyebrows arched like a pair of furry porticos, a smile pulling his thin lips taut.

"What are you talking about? What's fixed?" Dr. Bhandary asked, without even bothering to look up from the open panel she'd been tinkering with on the side of the ship.

"The sat-e-lite telecaster," Dr. Tanaka said, trembling with excitement. "The communications systems I've been working on for the past month. They're operational again."

Dr. Bhandary stopped what she was doing and stood. The rest of us gathered behind her like chickadees behind their mother hen. We were cautious in our optimism. We'd grown so acclimated to devastating news that anything else took a moment to translate.

"The telecaster is fixed," he said again, as if he knew we wouldn't believe him. "We can call home."

A bundle of wires extended from the ship to the rectangular device, feeding it just enough electricity to work. Slug slime coated the thing like a chrysalis, holding the various components in place, and keeping the antenna from toppling over. It smelled horrible, but it did the trick.

We stood behind him as he toggled one of the switches. The thing crackled like tin foil as it powered on. The Moonfellows let out a cheer. Dr. Tanaka put a finger to his lips. *Shush*. He needed to concentrate. This was our first phone call home. A lot could still go wrong.

"So what I've done is devise a sort of a coordinate-based *global positioning system* that utilizes a series of evenly dispersed latitudinal and longitudinal lines, the intersection of which correlates to a specific location within a kind of three-dimensional Euclidean space encircling the globe. It's a lot less complicated than it sounds. The Equator and the Prime Meridian both lay at zero degrees. The machine does most of the calculations by itself."

Dr. Tanaka punched a bunch of letters and numbers into the keyboard in front of him.

38 53 52. 6452 N 77 2 11. 6160 W
W-H-I-T-E H-O-U-S-E O-V-A-L O-F-F-I-C-E

He hit the enter key, and somewhere in orbit between the moon and the Earth the sat-e-lite whirred to life. The thousands of mirrored panels upon it tilted themselves at his command.

The screen lit up. A picture faded in. The Earth from a distance. Just a dot. Almost invisible against the darkness of space. Dr. Tanaka pressed the button with the drawing of a tiny magnifying glass on it. The telecaster clunked like a projector switching between slides.

The camera pulled in. Now we were focused on America.

Magnifying glass again. The image pulled in even closer.

The East Coast. The Mid-Atlantic. Washington DC.
Click.

Now onto Pennsylvania Avenue, with its cherry trees and tourists and Edwardian clad senator-types, briskly walking up and down the sidewalk like they had places to be.

Click.
Onto the White House itself.
Click.

DANGER SLATER

We were like Peeping Toms. Creeping up to the window on the West Wing. Our lusty sights trained on the Oval Office. Trained on the man who sat behind the desk, with his slick-backed hairdo and austere jawline and unlit cigar clamped between his teeth.

Even though the picture was in black and white and the resolution was not that sharp, I could still tell almost immediately that the man lounging in that office was *not* Archibald Eugene Harper III, the 26th President of the United States of America.

He was that shifty-looking liaison. From back in the warehouse days.

33.

"SURE YOU GOT the right office, Ken?" Dr. Bhandary asked.

"Yes I have the right office," Dr. Tanaka huffed, even though he was already in the process of double-checking his GPS coordinates. "My machine is so precise we could count the pimples on his face if we wanted to."

"I don't think he has very many pimples," said Dr. Chase. "His skin is exceptionally clear. Like it's made of wax or something. He's very handsome."

"Jeezus, Beth. I was being hyperbolic. I don't give a fuck about his pimples."

"And I'm just saying, he's a very handsome man."

"Maybe he's just keeping the President's seat warm for him?" I suggested.

The liaison kicked his feet up on the desk and touched a lit match to the end of his stogie.

"And maybe he's keeping the President's cigar warm for him, too."

Dr. Tanaka picked up the phone receiver from the side of the box and dialed up the Oval Office—a tangled 28-digit code—the rotary wheel clicking as it reset after each number. We watched him with bated breath. Like he was defusing a bomb.

"You can all relax. It's gonna work fine. That big ole antenna on top creates something I like to call a *cellular signal*. It uses the sat-e-lite as a relay node to amplify itself.

The telecaster should be able to transmit instantaneous auditory correspondence to anyone back on Earth with a receiver."

"So this whole thing is just a big phone then?" asked Dr. Bhandary.

"Essentially," Dr. Tanaka replied. "A little more advanced. A little bit smarter. Think of it like a *smartphone*, if you will."

On the telecaster screen, the liaison suddenly sat up and cocked his head at the telephone on the desk. It was as if he hadn't even noticed it until it started ringing. Not a lot of people owned telephones back in 1906. It was fairly uncommon to have anyone calling.

"Hello?" the liaison said, as he placed it to his ear. His insidious voice all too familiar.

"Hello. This is Doctor Kenji Tanaka, chief communications officer and electronics expert for the Moonfellow Program. I am calling from the lunar surface amid the ruins of the SELENE ONE spacecraft. It is of the utmost importance that I talk to President Harper at once."

"Harper?" the liaison scoffed. "Harper lost reelection. This is President Noah Martinson speaking. And did you say the Moonfellow Program? Is this a joke?"

" . . . President Martinson?" Dr. Tanaka said.

"Look, if this is the Canadian Prime Minister, just knock it the hell off. I'm glad you finally got a telephone installed, Geoffrey, but stop crank calling me."

"This is not the Canadian Prime Minister, sir. This is Dr. Tanaka. Of the Moonfellow Five."

"Impossible," Martinson said. "The Moonfellows have been dead for years."

Captain Mangrove let loose a thunderous groan. He'd been uncharacteristically quiet all afternoon. But now, it was as if something inside him had snapped. His skin was the color of a rotten banana and his black eyes were twisted in different directions at the end of their stalks. He writhed in agony, a monolith of murky and malodorous flesh. His breath was so heavy and wet it sounded as if his lungs had been liquefied.

"Wait . . . what do you mean we've been dead for *years*?" said Dr. Tanaka. It had been 36 days since we crashed on the moon. There hadn't been a moment unaccounted for since we'd arrived.

Mangrove started to cough. Wads of phlegm leaked from the slits of his nose.

"What year is it, sir?" My mouth had gone dry, but I managed to eke out the question, even though I wasn't sure I wanted to hear the answer. "Where the hell is President Harper?"

The liaison shook his head.

"Jeezus, Crumb. You're as clueless as ever. Today is April 14th, 1909. Harper's term was up. I ran against him. And I won. Where the hell have the five of you been? We terminated the Moonfellow Program nearly three years ago."

Three years ago?

Three fucking years ago?!

What did he mean? We'd only been on the moon for a month.

"I don't understand," said Dr. Chase. "There's gotta be a mistake. It doesn't even make sense. How could so much time have slipped by without us noticing?"

"*You're* the scientists," said President Martinson. "Aren't you the ones who are supposed to be telling me these things? What do you think we were paying you for? Or technically-speaking, I guess we weren't paying you per se, but you know what I mean. It's a turn-of-phrase."

"Sublunar-time dilation . . . " Dr. Bhandary mumbled to herself. Wide eyes darting back and forth, as if she were scribbling upon a chalkboard inside her head. "The math checks out. I wouldn't think it'd be possible, but it is. The numbers don't lie."

We turned to her. Even Martinson leaned in.

"What numbers? What are you talking about? What the hell is *sublunar-time dilation*?" Dr. Chase said the words like she was trying to spit the taste of them out of her mouth.

Dr. Bhandary held up two rocks. A big one and a small one. The Earth and the moon. She twirled them in each hand while having them rotate around each other while simultaneously pirouetting in circles herself. Three things spinning at once. Dr. Bhandary was the sun in this demonstration.

"It's the phases of the moon," she said, as she twirled. "See how it waxes and wanes in the shadow of the sun. But the thing is, time and space are relative to the observer. There is a cosmic dance happening around us. But most of the time you'd never know it. We spend so much of our lives standing in the same spot."

"I don't think I follow," said Dr. Chase.

Dr. Bhandary stopped spinning.

"It takes 29 days, 12 hours, and 44 minutes to complete one full lunar cycle. You can track the progress from your front porch. Each night the darkness grows until the moon disappears. And each night the darkness shrinks until it is dawn once again. It's how we built our calendars. The earth days surrounded by the lunar day, the month."

"So what are you saying? That time moves differently on the moon than it does on Earth?"

"That's exactly what I'm saying. By a rate of about 30 to 1," said Dr. Bhandary. "And since we've been marooned up here for 36 *lunar* days, that would mean . . . "

" . . . 1080 days have already elapsed on the planet below us," Dr. Tanaka said.

Dr. Bhandary nodded. "The aforementioned three years President Martinson just mentioned. Sublunar-time dilation."

All I could think about was Bella and Maxine. Now not

only was a great physical distance separating us, but also a growing schism of time. My family was rapidly drifting further away from me, and I had no way to stop it. Three years had already gone. Immense feelings of guilt overcame me. So much so I could barely breathe.

"Mr. President, sir, we've run out of food," Dr. Tanaka said. "And the MacGuffinite reserves have failed to turn up. There's nothing up here but dirt and slugs, sir. Even Captain Mangrove is . . . " she turned and looked at the seemingly catatonic human skin tube behind us, " . . . well, let's just say Captain Mangrove is having some *personal issues*. The situation is dire. Has a rescue mission been mounted? Is there an extraction plan in place? How are we supposed to get home?"

President Martinson leaned back in his chair and stamped out his cigar in an elephant tusk ashtray. From the box of Cubans to the left of him, he pulled out a new one and lit it up.

"Kenji, was it?" the President said, as a plume of smoke encircled his head. Dr. Tanaka nodded. President Martinson continued. "Kenji, listen, if you ask me, this whole MacGuffinite thing was a red herring from the get-go. I mean, what do we need this clean-burning space rock for when we got good ole fashioned American coal literally under our feet right here in the USA? I got elected on a platform of no-nonsense economic policy. Reduce government waste. Reinvest in infrastructure. Deregulate environmental sanctions. And let corporate profits soar. It's not revolutionary by any means. It's what the people want. It makes fiscal sense. So I cut unnecessary expenditures. The EPA. The Clean Air Act. And, of course, the ridiculously-overfunded and highly-inefficient space exploration project my predecessor set up. I saw firsthand how extravagant the Moonfellow Program was. And when your communications went out all those years ago, I saw it as a godsend. What an embarrassing and costly fiasco that was. Luckily, we launched in secret, just to hedge our bets. Hell, it was probably the only smart move we made at the time."

He reached into his desk and pulled out a thick file, holding it up for us to see. On it was written the words MOONFELLOWS—SUMMER 1906—TOP SECRET.

"This is the only remaining proof that you're up there. If something were to happen to this little folder here— *poof*—just like that, you'd be gone forever."

He tossed it into a nearby wastepaper basket and dropped his stogie in after it. The file caught fire. Smoke billowed up in the Oval Office. He pulled yet another cigar out of the box and lit it against the dancing flames. Mangrove wailed some more.

"The United States Government thanks you for your service," President Martinson said. He hung up the phone with a dramatic click.

Mangrove suddenly sat straight up. Like a reanimated corpse. His body was a twisted fusion of pulsating muscle and his deranged wide eyes rolled in our direction, hungry for blood. The Moon Flu had progressed to its Final Stage. He had become a 10-foot-tall slug monster. The transformation was complete.

He roared so loudly it nearly flattened the moonscape. And before any of us knew what was happening, The Thing That Was Once Captain Dirk Mangrove attacked.

34.

IT WAS LIKE a tidal wave. All fury and froth. Mangrove was moist with silvery mucus and his body rippled like there was something trying to punch its way out of his skin. He was snarling and screaming. Flexing and roiling. Insane. Angry. Animalistic. Out of control.

He barreled through us. Dr. Bhandary and Dr. Chase and I were tossed aside like bowling pins. I hit the ground several yards away, the impact so hard it sent a lungful of moon dust straight up my nose. I gasped for breath but found none there. My chest was a cement mixer. I dragged myself as far from the melee as I could. Tucked my head into my arms.

Mangrove moved like a wrecking ball. Like a giant fleshy fist. Wheezing. Howling. Each noise less human than the last. A creature governed only by adrenaline and madness. A hideous new species. A Slug-Man.

We all managed to get out of his way except for Dr. Tanaka, who only had enough time to reflexively put up his hands.

"Captain? Please stop! Captain, what are you doing?!"

He slammed into the electronics expert. The doctor was rendered helpless as Mangrove ejaculated ropes of pearly white slime all over him.

Momentum propelled the two of them forward. Dr. Tanaka trying to plant his feet. Trying to slow them down. But it was no use. Mangrove was just too big. Too determined. Too strong.

They crashed full-speed into the sat-e-lite telecaster. Sparks shot out of the side of the device like fireworks. The sky was illuminated with crackling light. Dr. Tanaka screamed in pain, his terrified voice cutting through the din like a knife. A wet squish. A bony crunch. A few desperate gurgles. And then a strange kind of silence quickly fell over the scene.

Dr. Tanaka looked down. Swallowed hard. The two-foot-tall "cellular" antenna had broken off the machine and was now poking out of the center of his chest. Blood pooled beneath him, mixing with the gray dust, thick like melted strawberry ice cream. His breath sped up. Sharp and fast. Like a hiccup.

"It appears that I've been impaled by my own invention," he said.

And then his eyes rolled up into his head and he expired.

Captain Mangrove sat back on his keel. A satisfied expression on his maw.

"The moon runsssss through me. It's inssssside my veinssssss." His voice was barely recognizable as a voice at all. More like a rumble. A vibration. An intrusive thought. "I've never felt sssssso powerful."

Away, he slunk. As fast as his newfound form would allow. Away from us. Away from the SELENE ONE. Away from the mess he made. Away from everything.

Mangrove crossed over the distant ridge.

To the dark side.

And out of sight.

90

35.

SLEEP DIDN'T COME that night.

I honestly doubted that sleep would ever come again.

The day left us withered like flowers thirsty for the rain. A sharp sniffle. A soft sob. It was all we could muster. Awake in the darkness. Lost among the stars. Mangrove could spring out at any moment. I think we all knew it. We were sitting ducks. We were totally helpless. By tomorrow morning, another two weeks on Earth would have passed. By this time next week, it would be half a year. No one knew we were up here. President Martinson waved his hands like a magician and *abracadabra,* in a puff of smoke we were gone. Nobody was coming to get us. Nobody cared.

At sunrise I took my shovel and found a good plot of land and we laid Dr. Tanaka to rest. We used the crooked antenna to mark his tomb.

A gravedigger's work was never done.

I said a few words. Not a proper eulogy, but a eulogy nonetheless. None of us knew Dr. Tanaka all that well. None of us knew each other all that well. But I did my best.

"Ahem. Well um . . . I guess, what can we say at a time like this? Kenji Tanaka was a scientist. He was born somewhere on Earth and died somewhere on the moon, a fate we're all pretty much doomed to endure. He had dark hair and stood about five and a half feet tall. I'm not sure if he had any family or not. I don't know if he had any friends or coworkers or pets or houseplants. He wasn't exactly forthcoming with a lot of personal information. But he was a nice enough guy, I suppose. I'm sure he had people who will miss him."

The hopelessness of our situation settled around us like the ash from a volcano. I wonder if Bella had given up hope, as well. Even if Higgins did as he promised and actually told her I said goodbye, at this point, Bella must have already grieved and healed and moved on. Life moves on. Life keeps moving on. The men in black simply showed up one evening and took me away. That was all the closure she had. I am haunted by these thoughts. If Maxine saw me today, she wouldn't even recognize my face.

"You guys!" Dr. Chase shouted, as the evening drew near. "Come over here and look at this!"

Dr. Bhandary and I walked over to where she was sitting. I could still see drops of Dr. Tanaka's blood in the dust around me. Dr. Chase had the broken sat-e-lite telecaster propped up against a rock. Once again, it had been split open. A complicated network of innards burst out of the chassis. The screen was covered in tiny cracks like a bulbous and bloodshot eye. The whole contraption buzzed like it was full of flies.

"It's garbage, Beth," Dr. Bhandary said. "We might as well have buried it with Tanaka."

"No, no, no, look." She moved the telecaster around a bit. A centimeter to the left. Another centimeter back to the right. Tongue out and brow furrowed in concentration. "I just gotta find the sweet spot," she said. "There we go!"

She took a step back and fell into line with Dr. Bhandary and I. The three of us surveyed her handiwork. The device still had a bit of juice in it. And the picture was still on.

The reception was poor. Distorted along the edges. Flickering in and out. Flakes of static appeared like a digital snowstorm across the scene.

We were looking at the Oval Office. The last coordinates the sat-e-lite had been set. Due to that sublunar-time dilation thingy, nearly a month had passed since yesterday.

Nobody was in the room except for a haggard maid, cleaning up a bunch of empty beer cans from what must have been a wild party held the night before. She had no idea we could see her.

"It works?!" said Dr. Bhandary.

"Barely," Dr. Chase replied.

"Well let's fuckin' call that maid then!" I said. "What are we waiting for?! An invitation?"

Dr. Chase motioned to the shattered telephone receiver. It lay in a thousand jumbled and jagged pieces. No more useful to us than a handful of confetti.

"Yeah, I don't think we're gonna be calling anyone anytime soon," she said. "As far as a communication device goes, this box is now completely defunct."

"Defunct?"

"You need to think of it less like a passageway and more like a window. We can look through it, but we won't be able to pass anything along. We can see them. But they can't see us."

The White House maid was on her hands and knees, picking up cigarette butts and used condoms and the rest of Martinson's Presidential trash.

"Jeezus, you're making it sound like we're some kinda ghosts, Beth."

"Yeah. Well. We kind of are."

I could feel a strange sort of pressure building within me. I wasn't sure how to explain. It was like my fingers were going to shoot off my body. Like high-octane anxiety coupled with a growing sense of dread. I pushed past Dr. Chase like she was nothing more than a saloon door. I sat in front of the telecaster. The keyboard before me was like some kind of cryptic puzzle box.

"How does this thing work again?" I asked.

"You have to put in the coordinates," Dr. Bhandary replied.

"But how do I figure out the coordinates?"

"You gotta use the latitudinal lines. Count up from the Equator. Then over from the Prime Meridian. If there are 360 of them encircling the globe and they're evenly-spaced apart, that would put one every 70 miles or so. He said the machine does most of the math for you. You just gotta know where you're trying to look."

I typed in N-E-W J-E-R-S-E-Y.

I typed in S-A-S-Q-U-A-H-A-T-C-H-E-E R-I-V-E-R.

I typed in L-O-N-E F-I-R C-E-M-E-T-E-R-Y.

I typed in H-O-M-E.

Clickity-clack went the buttons beneath my nimble fingers as the picture onscreen pulled away from the White House until we were back out in space, static steadily pulsing throughout the image like a heartbeat, the whole machine rattling like an engine low on gas. And then, slowly, the picture pushed back in again. The world got closer. To the East Coast. To New Jersey. To my house along the banks of the Sasquahatchee River, the jagged landscape of the city juxtaposed behind it like an open mouth with broken teeth.

I hit the magnifying glass button one last time. The feed pulled in even closer. I could see through the main window of my old home. Into the empty dining room. The last room I was in before the G-men came and took me away. Everything was there just like I remembered it.

Off-camera. A shadow. Moving along the edge of the screen. Someone was there, just out of view. My hands trembled as I adjusted the angle. The camera moved an inch to the right.

And there she was.

Bella.

My Bella.

Setting the table as it neared suppertime.

I felt as if I'd seen an angel. As if I'd been spontaneously cured of all diseases. As if I just did a line of physician-prescribed cocaine powder. Lithe and radiant on the telecaster screen, Bella shone brighter than any movie starlet I'd ever seen. My heart thumped in my chest. I was as in love with her as I'd ever been. My god. The tears welled up. The nearby moon slugs seemed to sense the water coming out of me and started climbing up my pant legs, trying to get to my face. I plucked the gastropods off and tossed them away like rotten berries.

"That's her." I was barely able to speak. "That's my Bella."

The two ladies standing over my shoulder were substantially less moved than I was.

"What is she holding there?" asked Dr. Bhandary. "Is that a pot of beef stew?"

A child joined Bella. No older than four. In pigtails, wearing a tartan dress and tights like she had just come back from church. She took a seat at the kitchen table.

Maxine. No longer a baby. A toddler. A little girl. I'd missed her first steps. Her first words. All of her firsts. By next week she'd be five. The week after that, six. And so on.

"Oh my god," I stammered. "She's gotten so big! She's a perfect doll!"

Bella ladled out a bowl of stew for the child. Then she ladled out a bowl for herself. You could even see the steam rising from it. I missed her cooking. She fixed a third bowl and placed it at the head of the table, in front of the empty chair that used to be mine.

"You see? She still puts a bowl out for me."

"Why would she do that?" asked Dr. Chase.

"I don't know. As a tribute or memorial or something? It's romantic."

"I don't know about that. It looks like there's someone else there."

95

"Huh?"

"Look, there's another shadow off to the left. Someone is coming in."

Enter a man. Tall and lanky. Square-shouldered. Brown-haired, neatly combed. This man wore a black suit, like a pallbearer, and moved through the house like he was already intimately familiar with it.

I recognized him immediately. As did Dr. Bhandary and Dr. Chase. We all knew this man.

It was Higgins. Higgins was in my house.

He rustled Maxine's hair before giving Bella a quick kiss on the lips. Then he sat down in *my* chair. At *my* dining room table. He picked up *my* spoon. And started eating *my* beef stew.

Dinner was served. All three of them were smiling.

From the dark side of the moon, I could hear Captain Mangrove. Snarling. Squishing. Raving to himself. A wereslug unable to find his human form again. The lunar light did not waver. His night was endless. As was mine.

I lay on my back in the moon dust. Ready and willing to join it forever. How could I go on? Why would I even *want* to go on? What else was there? What was the point?

"She left me," I whimpered to myself. "She left me for *him*."

And then a small hand was extended. Dr. Bhandary. Palm open. Above me.

"Take it."

"No."

"Take my hand and get up."

"I don't want to get up. Just leave me here. Just let me die."

"That's not how it works, Crumb. We're a team, remember? We're the Moonfellow Five."

"There's only three of us left."

"Fine then. We're the Moonfellow Three. The point is, things are lookin' bleak. But we're all in this together. And

96

if you end up dying on this stupid rock, well then so will we. So fuck Higgins. Fuck Harper. Fuck Martinson. Fuck whatever President comes next. Fuck the whole world and everyone in it. We're getting the hell out of here. And you're coming with us."

I linked my hand into hers. Used it to brace myself as I stood. I brushed the slugs off my jumpsuit. Dried my eyes. Wiped my nose on my sleeve.

"So do you—have a plan or something?" I asked.

"Not a very good one," she said. "But fuck it. What have we got to lose?"

36.

THE IDEA WAS SIMPLE:

Salvage what little materials were left of the SELENE ONE spacecraft and use the leftover parts to construct a smaller, secondary capsule. It wouldn't be much, Dr. Bhandary told us. It honestly might not even work, in the end. But it was also the only chance we had to get off the moon, once and for all.

We were gonna build an escape pod out of the scraps.

"There are only enough materials left for a single-rider vessel," Dr. Bhandary said. "And it's going to be pretty spartan. There will be very little control when it comes to steering this craft. We simply lack the components. What we're talking about here is more akin to a cannonball than a spaceship. And there will only be room for one of us inside."

"What does that mean?" I asked.

"It means one of us is going to hafta go on a suicide mission while the other two stay behind."

"What about fuel?" asked Dr. Chase. "Without MacGuffinite, how do we expect to get the capsule off the moon in the first place, let alone all the way back to Earth?"

"That's a problem I'm still trying to figure out," Dr. Bhandary replied. "What we need, ideally, would be a sort of giant catapult or slingshot or a centrifugal launching system. If we can figure out a way to propel this capsule upward with such a speed and at such a trajectory, then fuel and navigation won't matter. There is no friction in space. It's just gotta be headed in the right direction when we shoot it off the moon. And once it crosses paths with the Earth, gravity should take care of the rest."

"The Earth will catch it?" I asked.

"In theory, yes. Of course, this means the initial launch will have to be calculated just right. Basically, what we're trying to do here is hit a golf ball into a moving hole. And we only got one shot at it. If we miss the target, the pod will continue onward. Indefinitely. If our aim is just slightly off and it bypasses the Earth, it will be lost in space. Forever. Do you understand what I'm saying, Crumb?"

I didn't quite understand the science of it, no. But that was nothing new. I got the gist.

"Okay, so which one of us is going to go?" I finally asked.

"I—I'm not sure," Dr. Bhandary stuttered, as if she hadn't considered the question before.

There was a pause as we all looked from one to the other.

"I think it should be me," I finally replied.

Dr. Bhandary shook her head.

"I don't think you know what you're volunteering for, Crumb . . . "

"You're right. I don't know what I'm volunteering for. And I don't really care. You all have been so instrumental during our time here. And we'd already be dead if it weren't for the contributions of the two of you and Dr. Tanaka. Well, I never brought much to the Moonfellow Five. And I never found MacGuffinite. But I'd like the opportunity to finally pull my weight around here. For Dr. Tanaka. For my daughter and wife back home. And for the rest of you."

The scientists exhaled. Almost in unison. An argument was futile. Because they knew I was right.

Once again, a caterwaul could be heard. Vicious and wild. Reverberating across the chasm of darkness. Captain Mangrove in the shadows, the moon monster, wailing.

37.

DR. BHANDARY GOT to work. She stripped the SELENE ONE of its unessential parts and refashioned them into a secondary spacecraft. Smaller. No bells and whistles. No accouterments. Not even a toilet. If I had to use the bathroom I'd have to do it in a bucket. It was a simple escape pod, molded into a perfect sphere. An aluminum bubble. Airtight and impenetrable. Built just for me.

A safety belt was affixed to an unpadded plastic seat. Some insulation was haphazardly glued to the walls for warmth. A rudimentary steering system was installed, a single rudder attached to the back, controlled by a toggle stick poking out of the floor.

The thing was a death trap. It looked terrifyingly flimsy. Like it could fall apart in a stiff breeze. But I was confident in the skills of my fellow crewmates. I knew they wouldn't send me into harm's way if they could avoid it.

"Unfortunately, we really can't avoid it," Dr. Bhandary said.

"Oh," I replied.

To launch, we needed speed. A lot of speed. And as far as I knew, there was only one place on the moon we might be able to achieve it.

"A couple days ago, while I was making my rounds, Captain Mangrove and I came across this giant . . . hole in the ground. Or, not a hole, but like a . . . um, what was it called again when a meteorite causes a hole?"

"A crater?"

"Yeah, that's it. We came across a massive crater. About 20 miles east of here, right at the edge of where we were exploring. It was really steep on the sides, but you could see it start to curve and round out as it dipped into the darkness. Kinda like a bathroom sink."

"A bathroom sink?" Dr. Bhandary echoed me with incredulity, like she wanted me to hear it back so I'd know how stupid I sounded. But then I could see the gears start to click into place. "Wait a sec. A bathroom sink. From the meteor impact. Concave. Like a parabola. Like a big ol' ramp."

"Yeah, like a ramp," I said. "Exactly like that."

She was already lost in thought. Calculations whizzing through her head. Her eyes lit up.

"We'd have to see it," she said. "Make sure the angle is just right. But if the geometry were in our favor, then yeah, it might work. All we'd hafta do is push the capsule over the edge. It'd gain momentum as it rolled down the slope, hopefully picking up enough steam along the way to catapult itself off the opposite end and out of the lunar atmosphere. We point that sucker in the direction of Earth, and *voila*, it's a one-way ticket home. No MacGuffinite necessary."

"Easiest thing in the world," I said, with a wink.

"But Crumb, you realize you'll be *inside* this capsule as it's rolling into the crater, right? You're gonna get all banged up. You might not even survive the ordeal. At the very least it's gonna be uncomfortable in there. And claustrophobic. And not a very smooth ride. In fact, it's going to feel like you're in a coffin going over the edge of Niagara Falls."

I nodded. Yes. Okay. Fine. I didn't care. I knew there'd be danger. Danger is my middle name.

"We all end up in a coffin one way or another, Dr. Bhandary. I'd rather die fighting than live another 30 years wondering what could have been."

"Very well," she said. "Let's build you a coffin."

38.

A FEW DAYS passed on the moon, which meant a few more months passed back on Earth. And on the morning of the launch, I found myself feeling oddly wistful. Oddly nostalgic. I couldn't quite explain it. Perhaps it was just nerves. Or perhaps it was something else. I was about to leave this godforsaken place forever, and yet I couldn't help but feel that, in doing so, I would be losing something important. Like there was some part of myself that would always be left behind.

Dr. Bhandary suggested I take a few moments to myself. To both mentally and spiritually prepare for the journey ahead. Do some breathing exercises. Find my center. This was a practice she called *yo-ga* and apparently they'd been doing it in exotic places like India and California for thousands of years.

I found a quiet spot on the far end of the crater. My own little *yo-ga* studio under the sky. I could see Dr. Bhandary and Dr. Chase in the distance. Running through a few last-minute details. Tightening screws. Fastening panels. Rechecking the figures. Not a decimal point could be out of place. Against the black panorama of space, the two scientists looked so small. Like two tiny ants doing tiny ant work.

The escape pod was already set up against the yawning edge of the chasm, held back from the abyss by some flimsy scaffolding. Less than an hour to go before the ball dropped. It was like it was New Year's Eve or something. The countdown had already begun.

I was stretching my body and repeating my mantra—*there's no place like home, there's no place like home, there's no place like home*—when a sudden growl upon the breeze sent a shiver up my spine. Captain Mangrove. Still out there somewhere. As mad as ever. The dark side of the moon was his domain. Just beyond the ridge. Where the light never shined.

After Mangrove killed Tanaka, the rest of us remained on high-alert. We took up stones and pieces of scrap metal. Whatever weapons we could find. Ready to defend ourselves should the need arise. The captain's torturous and inhuman screams filled our evenings like the soundtrack from hell. But he never returned.

And once our fear of retaliation began to wane, a sense of sympathy soon took its place. Any one of us could have contracted the Moon Flu. Any one of us could have turned into a monster. Any one of us could have lost our minds. Captain Mangrove had a disease. And what he needed was help. I honestly doubt he *wanted* to hurt any of us. I can't imagine he actually *enjoyed* the multiple orgasms he experienced while all this violence was going down. He just lost control. It could happen to anyone.

"Mangrove?" I said, making my way up the summit. The shadows around me grew as I approached the peak. We never explored the dark side during our initial inquiries. We had no reason to. The moon was as barren as the most inhospitable desert back home. There were only the five of us and a bunch of random fucking slugs. There wasn't even any goddamn MacGuffinite. And once we learned about all this sublunar-time dilation crap, getting the hell out of here became our top priority.

I squinted into the darkness. From what little I could see, it was just as empty and boring as the rest of the lunar surface. When you looked up at the sky above it, the Earth and the sun were gone, completely obscured by the curve of the land ahead.

As my pupils widened, a few faint stars appeared within the black soup of space. Just a handful at first. Twinkling in the void. But as my eyes continued to adjust to the low light, a few more appeared. And a few more. And more. And more. And more. More stars, until the entire sky lit up like it was full of fireflies. The purple tentacles of the Milky Way unfurled, as wide as the horizon, embracing me and the moon and everything else in a kind of giant, celestial hug. This was the universe as I had never seen it before. Laid bare. Breathtaking in its naked beauty. I couldn't believe it. I was in awe.

But another wail soon stole back my attention. This one much closer, much more dire, than the last. It was almost as if these screams were coming up through the dirt. Everything seemed to vibrate in its wake. Captain Mangrove must've been in a seismic amount of pain. That was the only explanation I could think of as the terrain shifted around me like the sand in an hourglass. Suddenly, there was nothing for me to support myself on. The top of the ridge collapsed. The ground gave way.

In a cloud of dust, I tumbled down the far side of the escarpment. Rolling down the mountain. Into the dark.

39.

THE TEMPERATURE WAS much cooler down here. Just a few degrees above freezing. Like a night in late autumn. My breath appeared like a cloud in front of my nose. The starlight bounced off the white moonscape. I couldn't see well. Just enough to get by.

I sat up. To my left, the ridge lay partially collapsed. Dust piled up around me like I was sinking into the dune itself. To my right, the open plains, boundless and black. I scanned the horizon. It was as flat as a parking lot and as uneventful as an afternoon nap.

Except, wait a second.

There was something out there.

Or wait. No. There couldn't be. It was just a trick of the shadow. A pareidolia-type response somewhere in my lizard brain, like seeing the face of Jesus Christ on a piece of toast or something. This must be one of those Jesus-on-toast situations. The Son of God wasn't hanging out on your sandwich. Nothing was waiting for me on the dark side of the moon.

Or was there? What was that shape? Solid and stationary. Not a man or a monster or Mangrove moving through the darkness. Some sort of structure, perhaps? A house? A strip mall? A parking garage for UFOs? Or was it something else? Something even more incongruous? I was ill-prepared to find out. But then again, I was ill-prepared for most things.

I stood up and took an apprehensive step forward. I could see the structure was long. At least twenty yards from end to end. And it was tall too. A single rod stuck out of the center, with a second rod running parallel along the top. Kind of like a giant cross draped with rags. I could hear it flapping above the howls.

Another step. And another. Further onto this unlit plateau. Further from the ridge and the escape pod and everything else waiting for me on the sunny side.

My heart raced. My eyes widened until they nearly fell out of my head. I would've refused to believe any of this was possible had I not gotten close enough to lay a hand on its side. As unmistakable as my reflection. As real as my skin.

There was an old wooden Viking ship sitting next to me on the moon.

It was roughly the size of the SELENE ONE, though it obviously lacked any of our high-tech 20th-century gadgetry. No engine. No thrusters. No kitchenette. It looked like something out of the *Iliad* or fuckin' *Beowulf* or something. I didn't know much about boats. I didn't know much about classic literature either. But you get the idea. The ship was old. Overlapping planks of wood were held together by crude iron stakes. A dragon head was sculpted onto the bow, with rotten acorn eyes that once faced the ocean, but now pointed downward, towards the endless dusty lunar expanse. On the stern was a rudder, thicker than the tail of a whale.

The tattered remains of a red and white striped sail hung from the mast. It was apparent it had once been an impressive piece of fabric—intricately woven, sturdy and strong—but had long since degraded to almost nothing, set upon by both the elements and time.

A hole was torn in the hull. Wooden beams stuck out of it like cracked ribs. It appeared as if it scraped against a rock as it crashed, shattering in half in the process, perhaps suffering the same kind of structural failure that befell the SELENE ONE.

If I had to guess, I'd say this thing had been here for centuries. But how?

I looked around for clues but only found a few supplies strewn about, none of which seemed out of the ordinary. Hammers. Fishing poles. An actual worn-out copy of *The Iliad* by Homer.

"Ha, I knew it!" I said.

There was also a candle in a brass holder with a flintstone attached. I struck the flint against a nearby bolt and used the spark to ignite the end of the frayed wick.

Surrounded now by a small bubble of light. My own fiery little corona. And by contrast, the darkness beyond the candle's reach seemed to grow even darker. I could still hear Mangrove bellowing out there, but for the moment, at least, he sounded far away.

I ventured further. Through the gaping hull. Deeper into this mysterious ship.

The wood creaked beneath my feet. Slow and spooky. Magnified by the walls. I was reminded of being a little kid, back in my parents' cabin, along the east bank of the Sasquahatchee River, not far from where Bella and I would eventually settle down. This old boat sounded just like my childhood home as it shook under the wind of a summer's storm. Windows would rattle. Shingles would flap. The whole thing would feel like it was on the brink of collapse, ready to be taken by the sky.

It's just the man on the moon breathing, my mother would tell me.

My chest heaved in and out as I took another step forward and kicked something. It went sliding across the floor and thudded against the wall in front of me. I bent down and picked it up.

It was a leather-bound notebook. Or rather, some kind of diary. A personal journal. Cover faded. Spine cracked.

Coated with dust. This diary had seen better days, for sure. But it was mostly still intact, shielded from the harsher elements in the belly of this ship.

I unwound the strap and thumbed through the threadbare pages, until I got to the last entry.

Under the tangerine light of this single candle, I read:

I've often wondered what compels me to keep seeking out answers. To spite happiness. To spite reason. To spite everyone who told me I was wrong. I have always been brave. But ask myself now, what does that really mean? Perhaps I've been misled. Perhaps I am stupid. Perhaps fearlessness and foolishness have always been one and the same.

Coming to the moon was a mistake. I can see that now. I am alone and starving and in need of a rescue that I know will never arrive. I can only watch my planet from afar like a useless and forgotten god. My might and wisdom will be washed away in the tide of time. I fear this is the fate that has long since awaited me, the same pernicious fate that awaits us all.

I've already conquered the Atlantic, and all of the land on the opposite end. Vinland. And above. And below. And beyond. In many ways, the Earth was mine. But I still had questions. I still wanted more. And so I turned my sights upward. Toward the one direction us travelers only heretofore dreamed.

The moon sat as pregnant and full as she ever did. Curved like a woman. A beautiful maiden. And I coveted her and all the wonder that surely lay upon her shores. To be her first. To be her only. I was a man imbued with both bravado and hubris. Surely I deserved whatever I had the audacity to take. I vowed I would one day make the moon mine.

Of course, this was a journey with no known avenues. And conquering the moon would require a bit of ingenuity. But I am nothing if not resourceful. And the men in my employ are quite capable, as well. This was a problem we solved, as you can see. Though perhaps we solved it too well. Because I'm still here.

A long braided vine was strung between the peaks of two massive mountains. It was pulled taut and held in place at its vertex by a single tree. Betwixt these hills lie a dried-out riverbank that I had greased with the fat from 100,000 rams. The idea was when the tree was chopped, and the tension of the vine was released, it would act as a slingshot and propel the entire vessel forward, along this lubricated valley, hitting a ramp installed at the farthest end. Upward and outward. To the moon. Easy.

I had told my men that I needed a sturdy ship. A ship that could survive such an unconventional take-off. A ship that could sail across the blackest and most vast of seas.

Indeed, this ship has fulfilled half its promise. We launched at midnight, when the moon was at its apogee. A straight shot in front of me. A target impossible to miss. This vessel was spaceworthy alright, though perhaps not as impervious as we'd originally hoped. It broke apart upon landing. Shattering in such a way it made a return trip on it unfeasible. The moon is now part of my domain. But I had to sacrifice everything to achieve it. I feel time like the ocean itself, quickly flowing past me. Short of a miracle or divine intervention, I fear this is my final port.

I know not what the future has in store. My options seem to be dwindling. My food has run low. I've spent my whole life in pursuit of adventure. I've embraced the unknown. Beyond safety. Beyond comfort. Beyond even logic itself. I've often wondered if there was ultimate truth hidden behind the veil of this world. I suppose I shall find out soon. Regret is an anchor I cut a long time ago.

If this voyage is my undoing, then let me be undone.

The Diary of Leif Erikson
March 25th, 1021 AD

I lowered the journal and saw the skeleton in front of me. Slumped over against the wall. Collapsing into itself like a shitty old barn. The white bones were stained orange in the surreal light and the dual-horned helmet was still affixed to its head.

This was what was left of Leif Erikson's body. He died on the moon nearly 1000 Earth years ago.

This was too much. I simply could not comprehend. Vikings. On the moon. For a goddamn millennium. After all we'd been through, after all we'd been told, the Moonfellows were still just following in the footsteps of giants, this time beyond the stars, straight into the grave.

I tried to flip back a few pages but the ragged almanac was crumbling apart in my hands. Goddamn it. I needed to know more. More details. More information. More answers. Please.

creeeeeeak

The sound of weight on wood. I froze. Oh no. Because I didn't even need to turn around to know that he was already behind me. I could feel his breath like a knife on the back of my neck and was almost suffocated by the sour meat stench of his moldering flesh. Like the Angel of Death, he seemed to materialize out of the aether, the monstrous visage of my former captain, just inches from the tip of my nose. Pure madness. Pure chaos. Pure oblivion incarnate. He'd been poisoned by the moon and pushed beyond a cure. This moment was inevitable. Dirk Mangrove had found me.

40.

MANGROVE ECLIPSED THE hole in the side of the ship and blocked my only exit. A pillar of green-tinted mucus and muscle. Black eyes reflecting back my own terrified face. His mouth like a fleshy wound, full of razor-sharp blades where his teeth had once been. When he spoke, it sounded like his words were coming out of an industrial blender.

"He brought the slugsssss," the delirious captain said. His glutinous, pulsating frame seemed to suck in the darkness like a toke off a hookah pipe. The air around him felt corrupt. I couldn't tell where Mangrove ended and the twilight began. Fear paralyzed me.

"Wh—what?"

"Leif Eriksssson," the monster replied. "The sluggsssss ssssstowed away, in the bottom of his sssship. An infesssstation. He had no idea. They ssssslithered aboard, along for the ride, not knowing or caring where they were going. Or why."

He scooped a handful of gastropods off the ground with the stumpy tentacle that used to be his arm and shoved them all in his mouth. Guts and gore dripped down his puckered maw as he chewed. And when he swallowed, his skin bubbled with globs of fresh slime. He seemed to grow another inch in every direction.

"The slugsssss were the onesssss that colonized thissss planet. They're the onessss that discovered MacGuffinite.

And now I am their King. The moon issss oursssss. The moon issss mine."

"But there is no MacGuffinite. There is nothing here, Mangrove."

"We foolish men, little did we know, thissss has been their ssssstory the entire time. The slugsssss are the heroessss. The protagonistssss. The ssssurvivorsssss. They are the true heirsssss to the moon. They are the onessss who will be here after we're gone."

We were being swarmed by the slugs. It was almost as if they wanted Mangrove to eat them. He shoved more and more of them down his gullet. Flecks of half-masticated meat sprayed me like squalid rain. Slugs squirmed their way in and out of Leif Erikson's bones. Through his empty eye sockets. Under his ribs, where his heart used to beat.

"How do you know all this?" I asked him.

"Becaussssse I can hear them, Crumb," he replied. "The slugsssss. Inssssside of my head. They can talk to you, too, Crumb, if you're willing to lissssten."

"Please. Captain Mangrove. It doesn't have to be this way. We can get you out of here."

"I don't want to leave."

"We can get you help."

"I don't need your help."

Hulking in front of the gap in the Viking ship, Mangrove as immovable as a mountain. I could feel myself shrinking before him. Powerless. Little more than a slug myself.

"I—I have to go now, sir," I meekly said. "I'm going home."

He shook his head no.

"We don't leave the moon, Crumb. We *are* home."

And one of his goopy appendages shot out and struck me in the side of the head.

Vision blurred. Ears rang. Knees buckled. Pain wrapped around me like a blanket. The candle fell out of my hand and rolled across the floor. I landed next to the skeleton of Leif Erikson. His eyeless skull offered me no amelioration.

Captain Mangrove towered above me. Tail whipping up and down. I was struck again. And again. It felt as if my face was going to cave in. I couldn't fight back. Couldn't do anything at all besides curl up into myself and cower. My thoughts broke apart like a pane of glass. Blood leaked from my nose and mouth. Every part of me hurt.

The flickering flame cast the kind of light that made Mangrove seem even larger.

" . . . Thissss is where we belong, Crumb. Where we've alwayssss belonged. All of ussss. The moon wassss calling. And we anssssswered. The brave few. Like the Vikingssss. We are here to sssstay. If you cannot accept thissss, then I cannot let you go . . . "

He raised himself up. A sledgehammer. A wrecking ball. A man now ravaged by the Moon Flu. The last bits of humanity inside of him had been shed. There was no hope. For him. For me. For any of us. This was the end. He was going to destroy me. I was going to die.

I turned and blew the candle out.

41.

BUT HERE'S THE THING.

The candle didn't go out.

Instead, the flame spread. Across the bottom of the ship, so rapidly it almost stole the oxygen out of my lungs. Within a few seconds there was fire on all sides of me. Mangrove and I found ourselves suddenly trapped within the pyre.

The heat was intense and getting hotter. The Captain reeled back, shied away from the blaze, his animal instincts taking over, self-preservation outweighing his bloodlust.

The fire melted the soles of my shoes. I could feel my toes start to blister. I was badly beaten. I was barely alive. But Mangrove was distracted. This was my only chance to escape.

I slipped the Viking helmet off Leif Erikson's skull and put it on my head in a single and inelegant motion. Climbing to my feet, I charged forward like an angry bull, in the only direction I could. Directly at my former captain.

The horns sunk into his abdomen as he flailed backward and let loose a thunderous roar. He swung his tail at me again, but this time I ducked and scurried out of the way. It struck a support beam behind me and caused the fiery deck above us to cave in.

Burning planks of wood fell like flaming swords from above. I was hit in the shoulder but managed to stay on my feet. Fire licked the side of my face. It felt as if my eyeballs were going to melt out of my head. I turned away. Unable to breathe. Unable to bear it. And through the haze of smoke, I saw it. My opening. A new breach burned through the hull. A way out.

I dashed through and took off running.

The ship lit up behind me as the conflagration spread further. Across the deck. Up the sail. Wild flames kissing the sky. So bright I could now see like it was daytime. Yet the wailing of Captain Mangrove didn't fade. It only got louder. Angrier. As if the firelight were able to amplify his cries.

There was a crack like thunder as he burst out of the ship, sending blazing splinters flying in every direction. Some toothpick-thin. Others the size of oars. It was as if a bomb had gone off.

And Mangrove emerged from the smoldering rubble. Coming up behind me. Quickly gaining ground. The two of us in a mad and desperate dash toward the ridge. Toward my crew and our camp and whatever salvation was left for me.

I hit the base of the hill and tried to run up the slope. The whole thing crumbled around me and I lost speed. It was just too steep. I slid back down to where I began.

Captain Mangrove was tearing in my direction. A wave of destruction. Nearly here.

I was out of options. I had no clever ideas. I was not trained to fight monsters on the moon. I was just a gravedigger. I only knew how to dig. So I did what was sent here to do.

I dug.

Not down. But *forward*. Into the ridge.

I pulled handfuls of dirt out of the wall in front of me and threw them over my shoulder. Burrowing a tunnel through the moonscape itself. It wasn't reinforced, but the integrity held firm, the space just big enough for me to fit through.

Mangrove reached the far end. Grunting like a warthog, his open mouth dripping saliva, his alien teeth snapping. Ready to tear me to shreds. He squeezed himself into the opening. His body like jelly. Filling up the entire tunnel. Undeterred.

I dug as fast as I could. Kept pushing forward. I could feel the tips of my fingers becoming raw. Tearing open. Blood mixing with the dirt. I screamed but I didn't slow down until there was nothing left for me to dig. Eventually breaking through the soil. Emerging like a worm on the sunny side.

"He's coming! He's coming! He's coming!"

I shouted as loudly as my smoke-ravaged throat would allow. Nearly tripping over my own feet as I ran along the crater's edge. Back to my crewmates on the far end of the horizon.

Dr. Bhandary was busy securing the final few bolts on the outside of the beachball-shaped spacecraft. Dr. Chase was inside the pod, doing the same.

Mangrove burst out of the tunnel and continued the chase. The moon dust seemed to facilitate his movements. He was gliding like it were ice.

"He's coming!" I shouted again, but the two scientists were too engrossed in their work to notice me, charging their way, waving my arms, barking like a dog. "Run! Run away! Grab a weapon! *Do something*!"

Neither looked up until I was standing next to them, sweaty and crazy-eyed, hands braced against my knees as I wheezed out my warning once more.

"Run!"

"Jeezus, Crumb, you look like shit," said Dr. Bhandary. "I thought you were doing yo-ga. What the hell is going on?"

"It's Mangrove," I shouted. "He's right behind me. He's going to sabotage the mission!"

"Mangrove? What are you talking abou—?"

116

MOONFELLOWS

Eyes went wide with fear as she saw him. Captain Mangrove, no longer a distant threat, but an immediate one. An unstoppable human slug. A malevolent force of nature. Howling like a banshee. The impact was unavoidable. There was no time to think. Only react. I jump-tackled Dr. Bhandary and the two of us tumbled out of his path. She let out an *ouf* as we slammed against the ground in a gray cloud.

Mangrove leapt and missed us by only a few inches. His buggy eyes turned backward in disbelief as Dr. Bhandary and I rolled away. He tried to stop. Tried to slow down. But momentum kept him barreling forward. Toward the escape pod. Where the oblivious geologist was finishing her work.

Dr. Chase poked her head out of the hatch. Unaware that Captain Mangrove was right there.

"Is that you wheezing like that, Kari? Don't tell me you caught a cold."

Mangrove slammed into her. Hard. And the force of it sent them both stumbling backward into the tiny escape pod. The door swung closed behind them. The wooden pylons that kept it stable on the precipice bent and strained under the additional weight.

Blood splattered against the porthole as Mangrove tore into her. With the door sealed shut, we could barely hear Dr. Chase screaming. It sounded like she was already a million miles away.

The escape pod rocked back and forth. Back and forth. Dr. Chase struggling to keep the ravenous Captain off her as the whole contraption teetered on the lip of the crater. And then a *crack* as the pylons broke away. The docking station collapsed. The capsule tipped forward.

It careened down the side of the basin. Rapidly picking up speed. The off-tempo *thump thump thump* of Mangrove and Bethany's unsecured bodies bouncing around inside of it like pinballs. More blood on the porthole. More screaming. Hitting maximum velocity right at the lowest point before rocketing quickly up the other slope. They crested over the opposite lip and the capsule was launched like a cannonball. Straight up into the sky. Out of the lunar atmosphere.

In a blink, they were gone. Disappeared in the distance. Into space.

The entire process worked exactly the way Dr. Bhandary said it would. The calculations were spot on. The pod was constructed just right. Everything was perfect. Except for one small detail.

"They went the wrong way," said Dr. Bhandary.

"What?"

"The escape pod wasn't aimed at the Earth."

"What do you mean? What was it aimed at then?"

Her eyes were damp but somehow she managed to hold back the tears.

"Nothing," she said. "Endless nothing."

42.

THERE'S THIS RECURRING dream I have, whenever I lay down to rest. On the backside of my eyelids I'll find it, playing on a loop in my head.

In this dream, I have turned everyone on the Earth into wood.

I'm never quite sure how I pull this off. Whether it is a meticulous process or an instantaneous one. But the end result is always the same. Each individual has a new wooden body. Lacquered and shellacked to keep from rotting. Mouths like nutcrackers. Doll eyes affixed to the sky.

None of them can move. But they want to. And I know I must help them. This is a sacred task, bestowed upon me by some unknown force, as innate as hunger, as irrepressible as an itch. It is something I must do whether I want to or not. I must give these people life. I'm the only one who can.

I pluck all the hairs from my head. One by one. Until my scalp is as smooth as an ocean stone. This is a sacrifice I have made for them. My youth. My time. My body. All of me. My hair once grew thick and bountiful. Now it is just a pile in my hands.

I drape these hairs from the side of the moon. They fill the sky like jellyfish tentacles. Thousands of them. Millions of them. Hanging down. Enough to loop through the hands and feet of all the wooden people below me.

DANGER SLATER

The entire planet is strung up like marionettes. And I control the strings. I can make them stand. I make them dance. I can make them fall in love. And I can break their hearts. I am doing my best, though I often fall short. Nobody understands how their universe works. Not even me. But they don't have to understand the world to be grateful.

Even if they're sad, they can still be grateful.

43.

FOR THE NEXT few months, I sat glued to the telecaster screen. It was the only blessing I had left. My final tether to the Earth. To the life I once knew.

Neither Dr. Bhandary nor I talked very much. At least, not during this time. I suppose we were both in mourning. Not just for the other Moonfellows, but also for ourselves. The moon was haunted. And we were the ghosts.

The fuzzy low-res images of my loved ones flickered in front of me.

Maxine brushed her hair.

Bella kneaded some bread.

Unexceptional moments when taken alone. But together they form a much grander picture.

Dare I blink and days would pass me by. Should I take a nap and I'd lose a few months. But when I looked at the screen and focused on my family, time seemed to slow itself down to an observable speed. It was like watching a movie. These scenes cut together. I couldn't quite understand it.

I asked Dr. Bhandary if the machine had some kind of mechanism inside to compensate for the disparity. A *sublunar-time-adjustment-module* or something. But she shook her head no.

"Time moves through us. Not around us. It's not the machine, Crumb. It's your *perception*. I've spent my whole life searching for answers. But the only thing I've learned is that the rules we're given are not unshakable. Math. Physics. Science. Engineering. Everything you've ever accepted as the truth. They're all just stories we tell ourselves. Same as any other."

And like a masochist, I would return to the telecaster, again and again and again and again. My former planet. My former home. My former family. No longer mine:

Bella and Higgins held hands and went for a walk along the Sasquahatchee River. Following the same paths she used to walk on with me. They were lovers in the height of romance. He seemed to treat her right. He seemed to be a good man.

Maxine started kindergarten. She had on the romper Higgins had bought her. The proud stepdad sent her off with an affectionate wave, like *have a good day, honey, make lots of friends.*

Christmas morning arrived and the three of them exchanged gifts by the fireplace as the snow slowly fell outside. Frost formed on the windows. I could no longer see through it.

A ship called the *Titanic* hit an iceberg and sank into the Atlantic.

There was a World War and things got pretty bad.

Martinson lost his reelection and a new President took over—a man I did not recognize and who would not recognize me. He put his feet up on his desk and chomped his cigar. Just like his predecessor. And his predecessor before him. The latest in this long line of wannabe kings.

There was a *second* World War and things got even worse.

Black smoke poured out of the factories downtown. Ships from the bay carried in more and more people. Skyscrapers were built. Ghettos abound.

Another President was elected.

And another.

And another after that.

And I thought to myself, all these assholes kind of look the same.

Time was slipping by without my consent. I would stay awake forever if I could. I had to keep watching the screen. It was the only way to slow things down. I wanted to preserve my wife and daughter for as long as possible. But every morning when I woke up, I found myself thrust further into the future. The decades piled up around me like rubble in a junkyard.

Good god, is Maxine getting married already?!

Are those wrinkles that have settled themselves upon Bella's brow?

The cabin where I grew up was bulldozed and luxury waterfront condos were erected in its place. The sprawl of the city seemed to have no end. It covered the landscape like a fungus. More factories were built. This one manufactured disposable toothbrushes. The one next to it produced those little plastic tabs they use to tie bread bags shut. Smog replaced the air. Effluvium filled the water.

A filmmaker by the name of Stanley Kubrick staged a fake moon landing on some studio backlot. It looked realistic enough. People certainly seemed to buy it. Been there. Done that. There was nothing of interest on the boring ole moon. Best move onto Mars or Jupiter or whatever dumb planet came next.

And one night I woke up to the anemic glow of the telecaster screen flooding into the SELENE ONE and I thought for sure it must have been a malfunction. I knew I hadn't left it on when I went to bed. Perhaps there had been a short circuit or something. Perhaps it was on the fritz.

I climbed out of my cot and toward the light, and there I found Dr. Bhandary knelt before it. Hair in disarray. Big bags under her eyes. She must have woken up at some point and turned it on. She thought she was alone. She didn't hear me behind her. She once called the telecaster a high-tech torture device. But now, she watched it with the same kind of quiet intensity I often did.

On the screen, there was a man. Handsome. Tall. In a three-piece suit. He looked very important. Very suave. Perhaps only a few years older than Dr. Bhandary herself.

He ran through his innocuous morning routine. Sipped his tea. Ate his toast. Checked the time on his wristwatch before heading out the door. We watched as he took a seat on the local trolley. He must have been on his way to work.

"His name is Vihaan," she said, without looking my way.

"Your husband?" I asked.

"Ex-husband," she replied, as I took a seat next to her.

Vihaan read the newspaper as the trolley made its way across town.

"We had plenty of good moments," she said. "But we fought a lot, too. I don't know. It all seems so distant now. All my memories feel like I imagined them. Like they were all a part of some elaborate fantasy I had built for myself." She sniffled. Took a deep breath. "In a lot of ways, I kinda prefer it on the moon. Our problems out here seem so . . . *pragmatic*. When I look at my old life and I think about all the things left unsaid, it feels like a river trying to erode me away, leaving a gorge so deep I don't think I'll ever be able to cross it."

A tear rolled down her cheek. I didn't have words of wisdom to impart to her. Nothing clever to say. I simply gave her hand the slightest of squeezes, as if to tell her, you're not alone.

Maxine had a baby.

Grandma Bella took up gardening.

Higgins' heart gave out on his way to pick up the mail. Bella found him face down in the front yard. They buried the former government agent at the Lone Fir Cemetery. There was a plot in the ground reserved next to his. I knew for whom it was ultimately held.

MOONFELLOWS

When Bella passed, it was in her sleep. She was very old. She didn't suffer much.

And a similar fate befell Maxine. Perhaps a lunar year later. I didn't know the exact date. She was an old lady herself by then.

My family were strangers to me. But I loved them all the same.

And time kept passing. And the world kept spinning. And I wondered to myself, what year was it, anyway? Did anybody know? Did it even matter? 1942? 1996? 2016? 2063? 2115? 2486? 2687? 2883? Everyone I've ever known had been dead for centuries. Even the names on their headstones had long since faded away. Our ship crashed on the moon nearly 900 years ago. Give or take a decade or two. Nobody was really keeping score.

And at some point, Dr. Bhandary leaned over my shoulder. So close I could feel the soft tickle of her breath on my skin. She too had gotten older. As had I. Wrinkles pinched the corners of the engineer's eyes and silver streaks ran through her once obsidian hair.

She switched off the telecaster and yanked one of the vacuum tubes out of its side. She tossed it away like it was radioactive. I heard it shatter somewhere in the distance as the box powered down.

Before I could protest, she handed me a beaker of melted-down slugwater. She gave me a nod and I took a big sip. My hunger quickly fell away as the intoxicating effect of the drink blossomed in my belly. I felt as if a spell had been broken. As if I had just woken up.

"C'mon, Crumb," she said. "Let's go look at the stars."

44.

AND SO THE moon was free of monsters. And I was free from responsibility. It was as if a weight had been lifted from my shoulders. Yeah, it felt good to not have to be your savior.

One day, Dr. Bhandary asked me to collect some rocks and some dust and whatever debris I could find. She said she wanted to build out the wreckage of the SELENE ONE. She said she pictured it with buttresses as wide as shoulder blades and spires that stuck up like long, lean fingers. We were here for the long haul. We could do whatever we wanted. And she told me she wanted to turn our claptrap into a castle.

I picked up my shovel and headed out to the flats. This time to the west. I seldom ventured this way before the mission fell apart. There was still a lot of the moon that remained unexplored.

I started to dig and hit something almost immediately. Under the dirt.

tink

Like the sound of tapping on glass.

tink

My shovel rapped against it once more. No, I wasn't mistaken. There was something down there. But what could it be?

tink tink tink tink

I knelt and pulled out another couple of scoops until I

revealed what looked to be a giant sheet of ice. It was crystalline and incandescent. Like a diamond. But brighter. Harder.

Holy shit.

It was MacGuffinite.

I finally found it. After all this time.

The reflection of the sun bouncing off it was so bright I had to look away. Like a billion-watt searchlight cast directly into the sky. So radiant it was as if the moon were emitting lasers. It had to be conspicuous. Even from Earth. MacGuffinite aglow. Their salvation like an EXIT sign in a smoke-filled building. I wondered if there was anyone still down there left to see it.

I spent the rest of the day excavating as much of it as I could. Not because it would do us any good. But because I knew, in its sad way, it was once important somehow.

I dug out a ditch. Exposed a strip of MacGuffinite a hundred miles long. Then I dug two more ditches. One above it and one below. When I was finished, it looked like a giant, luminous letter I.

But I didn't stop there. I had more letters to carve. One after another. I wrote my epitaph. Generations must have passed as I did this. Not quick enough for a single person to notice in their lifetime. But slowly, my words began to appear. And by the time I was done, it was so big and bright that it lit up the whole side of the moon like a billboard.

If you look up, you might see it. My final message home.

It simply read:

I'M SORRY

And each night I would make my way back to the SELENE ONE with whatever materials I could scavenge and Dr. Bhandary and I would use them to build our castle, one brick at a time.

And when I was done, I would drink my fill of melted slugwater and let that two-flutes-of-champagne buzz settle into my bones. Yes, it smelled like rotten eggs and tasted like dog shit and once a week a cloudy yellow sludge would purge itself out of both ends as my body flushed itself of any excess toxins, but this was a perfectly natural process, Dr. Bhandary assured me as she filled her slop bucket with another round of excreta. A day of vomiting and diarrhea sure beat succumbing to the Moon Flu. Things could be worse. Things could always be worse.

I sometimes wonder what would've happened if the Moonfellow Program never existed. I like to think Dr. Bhandary and I would've still been friends. Like fate or something would've brought us together no matter what. I don't know. Maybe her and Vihaan would've gotten back together. Maybe they would've moved in next door to Bella and Maxine and me. Maybe we would've all ended up living in a cul-de-sac somewhere, our own little sat-e-lite, somewhere out in the suburbs. Maybe we all would've gotten jobs at that disposable toothbrush factory. Maybe we would've had backyard barbecues on the weekends. Maybe our kids would've gone to school together. Maybe we would've been happy.

These weren't greedy fantasies. They were the kinds of fairy tales people told themselves all the time. Most folks take their comfort for granted. All I ever wanted was a normal life.

And so Dr. Bhandary and I spent the rest of our days lounging on the patio of our moonlit castle like two tourists on the beaches of Ibiza. We were on a permanent vacation on an exotic foreign shore. We clinked beakers and slurped down our sluggy cocktails and stared out at the crater that stretched before us so wide it almost looked like an ocean. As dark below as the sky above.

I told her that Captain Mangrove forgot to give the crater a name all those years ago.

She told me she wanted to call it the Sea of Deliverance.

When I asked her why, she said she'd rather show me

instead. So she took me by the hand and led me toward the hole. Gigantic and black and terrifying and beautiful. We sat on the edge and dipped our toes into the abyss and Dr. Bhandary said that being here in this moment together would be the closest thing the two of us would ever have to a home.

The End

ACKNOWLEDGMENTS

Perhaps you noticed, but there is not one shred of "real" science in this book. This is by design. Go read *The Martian* if you're looking for a meticulously-researched outer space survival story. *Moonfellows* is intended to be much more allegorical in nature, and adherent only to its own internal logic. The film *A Trip to the Moon* (1902) by George Méliès was the jump-off point for me. They had no idea how cosmology or space travel worked back then, and as such, there is more imagination on display in that 15-minute 120-year-old movie than in most modern blockbusters. I love it. Other direct influences include *The Little Prince* by Antoine de Saint-Exupéry, *The First Men on the Moon* by HG Wells, *Star Trek: The Original Series*, and pretty much everything Kurt Vonnegut Jr. has ever written.

Big thanks to my girlfriend Constance Ann Fitzgerald who heard every idea in here (and then some) throughout the writing process. And huge thanks also to Max Booth III and Lori Michelle (my editors and publishers) without whom this book as you hold it in your hands would not exist. Other thanks to John Skipp, Rose O'Keefe, Michael Allen Rose, Garrett Cook, Daniel Barnett, Lisa LeStrange, and SG Murphy. Y'all contributed to this in one way or another, whether you're aware of it or not.

ABOUT THE AUTHOR

Danger Slater is the Wonderland-award winning writer of *I Will Rot Without You* and several other books that didn't win awards. You can find him on Twitter @Danger_Slater

The Perpetual Motion Machine Catalog

Antioch | Jessica Leonard | Novel

Baby Powder and Other Terrifying Substances | John C. Foster | Story Collection

Bone Saw | Patrick Lacey | Novel

Born in Blood Vols. 1 & 2 | George Daniel Lea | Story Collections

Crabtown, USA:Essays & Observations | Rafael Alvarez | Essays

Dead Men | John Foster | Novel

The Detained | Kristopher Triana | Novella

Eight Eyes that See You Die | W.P. Johnson | Story Collection

The Flying None | Cody Goodfellow | Novella

The Forest | Lisa Quigley | Novel

The Girl in the Video | Michael David Wilson | Novella

Gods on the Lam | Christopher David Rosales | Novel

The Green Kangaroos | Jessica McHugh | Novel

Invasion of the Weirdos | Andrew Hilbert | Novel

Jurassichrist | Michael Allen Rose | Novella

Last Dance in Phoenix | Kurt Reichenbaugh | Novel

Like Jagged Teeth | Betty Rocksteady | Novella

Live On No Evil | Jeremiah Israel | Novel

Lost Films | Various Authors | Anthology

Lost Signals | Various Authors | Anthology

Mojo Rising | Bob Pastorella | Novella

Night Roads | John Foster | Novel

The Nightly Disease | Max Booth III | Novel

Quizzleboon | John Oliver Hodges | Novel

Scanlines | Todd Keisling | Novella

SPOOKY TALES FROM GHOULISH BOOKS

PERPETUAL
MOTION
MACHINE
PUBLISHING

Patreon:
www.patreon.com/pmmpublishing

Website:
www.PerpetualPublishing.com

Facebook:
www.facebook.com/PerpetualPublishing

Twitter:
@PMMPublishing

Newsletter:
www.PMMPNews.com

Email Us:
Contact@PerpetualPublishing.com